Is it real or is it fantasy? That's the question MISix Agent Mathilda Honoria Spencer struggles with on her latest assignment. Tasked with discovering the whereabouts of Lady Annabelle Trask, Tillie is thrust into a world of Hucows and other human animals. It's a world that raises serious questions about sexual fetishes, intentional physical enhancements, and even pornography, but in the end, Tillie has only one mission—to rescue and return Lady Annabelle to the Queen. However, as she and her partner, Agent Abdul Ali, attempt to find Lady Annabelle and keep her out of the clutches of terrorists bent on destroying the monarchy, they must also wrestle with their feelings for each other. Can they draw the line between their duty to the Crown and their relationship with one another? Or must they embark on separate paths to continue to serve the Queen?

Bovine Tricks
Copyright © 2021 Seelie Kay
ISBN: 978-1-4874-3236-2
Cover art by Martine Jardin

Published by eXtasy Books Inc or
Devine Destinies, an imprint of eXtasy Books Inc

Look for us online at:
www.eXtasybooks.com or www.devinedestinies.com

Bovine Tricks
Royals Gone Rogue 1

By

Seelie Kay

DEDICATION

For those who have suffered not for who they are, but for what others believe they have failed to be.

CHAPTER ONE: WHEN THE LADY IS A COW

Mathilda Honoria Spencer—called Tillie, for short— placed her binoculars on a nearby rock and took a long sip of water from a sports bottle.

In a posh British accent, she said softly, "I don't know, sir. The only humans I see are men—farm workers, I suppose. I haven't seen a single female, except for cows, that is." She giggled. "And I couldn't tell a male cow from a female. I was raised in Gunnersbury. The only cows there were middle-aged women."

Tillie intentionally spoke distinctly. There was no hint of her youth—spent in a working-class neighborhood that dropped t's and h's as a matter of course. Tillie had worked hard to refine her speech and had learned to speak in the polished Queen's English. Her latent Cockney accent came to light only in times of extreme stress or when she was under-cover.

Her earpiece squawked. "Well, as it happens, you are looking for human cows. *Female* ones. Did you not understand the assignment?"

Tillie grimaced at the offense to her ears. The new communications devices MISix used were groundbreaking, but the squeaks and squawks delivered to the inner ear were most unpleasant. She blamed it more on the careless user than the device. She tapped on her earpiece. *Take that, you wanker.* "I know what was reported, but all of my research points to a big old modern-day fantasy. Human cows are a myth. They have to be. There is no other explanation. Someone is pulling our legs." She sighed. "What a waste of our time." She picked up her binoculars again. "I will give it another hour, then I'm coming in."

The man at command grunted. "Actually, Agent Spencer, after an hour you will be taking a closer look. You will sneak onto the farm and *investigate*. We have a confirmed report that there are Hucows on the premises and one of them is a member of the royal family. The Firm wants her found and extracted as soon as possible. It is our sworn duty as members of MISix."

"I think MIFive is better suited for something like this." Tillie's voice assumed a bit of snark. "After all, it's domestic. We are only responsible for international activities that threaten our citizens. This certainly does not apply." Tillie was well aware her tone was bitchy, but for crying out loud, here she was, in the middle of Devon, watching cows. She was much better suited to issues involving international sex slave trafficking and other forms of forced servitude. While rescuing members of the royal family had become her specialty, operating on domestic soil was risky. Given her fondness for high society events, she could be recognized and her cover would be blown.

"Except this is right up your alley. We suspect it *is* about slave trafficking. And it *is* international. If what has been reported is true, this farm is operated by an American corporation that specializes in trafficking young women in the fetish world, in particular, human cows, pigs, cats, dogs, even horses. Their buyers come from around the world. When matters cross borders, it falls within *our* jurisdiction."

Tillie scrunched her nose. "Why do we always get the cases that are so repugnant? If people are interested in screwing animals, why don't they just . . ."

"Because, Agent Spencer, bestiality or animal abuse, is a crime. However, there is nothing *criminal* about humans who dress up as animals and engage in sordid activities based on fantasy. That is, unless they are forced into it to satisfy someone's prurient interests. In the case of Lady Annabelle Trask, we do not know if her participation *is* voluntary. We have heard that she has undergone a rather extreme physical transformation, possibly in America. That *may* be a crime. We may be looking at a case of involuntary maiming and mutilation."

Tillie grimaced. "What sort of transformation? It's not like you can transform a human into a cow, or God forbid, breed a human and a cow."

Her superior emitted a long-suffering sigh. "I am well aware you were provided with photos and videos, Agent Spencer. Did you not peruse them?"

"Of course, I did," Tillie snapped. "I just thought it was some sort of porn, and everyone knows that stuff is photoshopped. I mean, there were women hooked up to goat milkers, their teats hanging to the ground. Not only is that obscene, but I would argue that it is a physical impossibility."

"Is it?" he asked softly. "Plastic surgeons might argue with that. They have been known to produce women with all sorts of physical anomalies. They can transition a man into a woman and vice versa, so why couldn't they transition a human into an animal, or the very least, make them look like one?"

"That's just sick. *Really* sick. No right-thinking man or woman would submit to becoming an animal." She shuddered. "I can't believe anyone would go that far."

"Well, as you read, we have received reports of at least twelve women currently being transitioned on that farm. One way or another, they have developed udders. They are milked daily and forced to behave as heifers. Then they are abused sexually. Some are used for breeding and their babies are sold on the black market. Some produce breast milk, which is also sold on the black market. Others are traded freely at private auctions for sexual exploitation. My God, some even *moo*."

Tillie peered through her binoculars. "Sir, I'm telling you, all I see down there are cows and they all appear to be, well . . . bovine."

The man fell silent for a moment. "If we can't find sufficient evidence to conduct a raid, we may need to insert you into the process. I suggest you get as close as you can and take a look around. Otherwise, you may be going in as a prospective Hucow."

Tillie gasped. "Are you fucking kidding me? There is no way I am going undercover and risk being transitioned into a cow or a pig or chicken. You can't ask me to take that risk."

Her superior chuckled. "Still think it's a myth, Agent Spencer?"

Tillie felt her blood run cold. She had been asked to do some crazy things and put herself in dangerous, life-threatening situations. But this was unacceptable. "Look, I've already gone above and beyond for MISix. I was kidnapped by a sex trafficking ring. Then I infiltrated a cult and spent six months in the Peruvian jungle, serving as one of the leader's sex slaves. And I was the target in that false imprisonment scam, at the behest of the Yanks. I was the one who went undercover to rot in a prison. I have performed well in each assignment. I don't deserve this."

"Did it ever occur to you that Her Majesty has personally requested your services? *Again*, I might add. It is a matter that requires the utmost discretion. We don't know if this royal is playing out some fantasy as a cow, has been forced into pretending to be a cow, or has been enslaved and turned into a cow. All of it is unsavory and the Queen wants it dealt with. She wants her relative extracted and returned to the human world. We don't know if she is there willingly, but most certainly, some sort of psychological rehabilitation will be involved. And if there has been a physical transformation, the Crown will have even more problems. This matter simply cannot be exposed to the public. The rags will have a field day. And the anti-Monarchists will use it to prove the royals are unfit to lead due to mental defect." He added, "If you fail, this could topple the Monarchy."

"Oh, bloody hell," Tillie muttered. "So even if I'm buried up to my eyes in pig *shite*, I need to make sure I come out smelling like a rose."

"Exactly."

Tillie tossed her binoculars on the desk of her superior, Lord Alfred J. Ryder. "I saw nothing untoward at the farm, and I got as close as I could without attracting attention. I have asked for hourly satellite sweeps. I couldn't get into the barns and stables. I don't know what else I can do."

She plopped down into an armchair and released her long hair from a large barrette, then shook it out and sighed. She was only thirty, but after kneeling on the cold ground for hours, she felt more like fifty. Her knees were stiff and sore. She needed a long, luxurious bath. The kind her lover, Abdul Ali, was fond of providing. Too bad he was in Morocco investigating the death of their arch nemesis, Prince Mustapha.

Mustapha had been a slave trafficker until he was blown apart by multiple bullets and other forms of munitions. When the Brits were blamed, Abdul had been called in to smooth things over. She was sure the Yanks were behind the Prince of Evil's death. They certainly had good cause. But they had not accepted responsibility. In fact, they had claimed other countries had more reason to assassinate Mustapha, and the press had bought it, running a number of stories analyzing *the facts* and pointing a finger at the Commonwealth. That had put the royal family in the middle of another scandal they could not afford.

Tillie sighed. No hot baths awaited her this evening. She stretched her legs. "So, I guess we wait . . ."

Lord Ryder frowned, and his abnormally fluffy white eyebrows waggled.

That was not a good thing. The waggle meant he was up to something. Something that usually put Tillie in danger.

He opened a drawer and pulled out a large white envelope.

Tillie smirked, "A wedding invitation, sir?"

He chuckled. "An invitation, yes. A wedding? Not exactly." He handed her the envelope.

Tillie gazed at it and read what was inscribed on it. "What is the *L'Academie des Paturages Humains*? I've never heard of it."

"In English, the Human Pasturage Academy. Pasturage is the process of acquainting domesticated animals, or in this case, humans, with grazing."

Tillie's eyes rounded. "What? They have a school for that?"

Her superior nodded. "I am afraid so. Not only do they teach humans to graze, or otherwise acquire animal characteristics, but they also offer a variety of human husbandry courses. Basically, many of the same techniques taught in animal husbandry, with a twist."

"Is that even legal?"

"Teaching it? Yes. Executing it? It's illegal only if the human is being forced to participate against their will."

Tillie shook her head. "What human in their right mind . . ."

Lord Ryder clucked his tongue. "My, my, aren't we the intolerant one? Tell, me, when Agent Ali had you on a leash while undercover for the Gibraltar affair, how did you feel?"

Tillie thought back to that mission. Prince Mustapha had called the women he enslaved *pets*. He had even called them *kittens*. They were led around on a leash, and sometimes were required to crawl on all fours and sit on a pillow at the feet of their master. Some were even fed from bowls set on the floor. Tillie shuddered. Mustapha had kept all of his pets naked, with large tails firmly planted in their arses. "It was humiliating. Demeaning. I hated it."

"And the power exchange? Giving up control to someone else?"

"Agent Ali was quite bossy. It was unpleasant."

The man smirked. "For a headstrong woman like you, I imagine it was. But some women *and* men actually enjoy giving up control. Especially in matters regarding sexual relations and the games they may play in the bedroom. Would it surprise you to learn that pet play is big business? Some people pay a lot of money to keep their human pets in comfort. Diamond collars, gold tails, custom-made cages, grooming amenities . . ."

Tillie pursed her lips. "I simply cannot imagine allowing anyone to humiliate me like that. Or to treat me that way. Their self-esteem must be in the sewer to permit that sort of degradation."

Lord Ryder tilted his head and studied her. "On the contrary, my dear. Some people enjoy being treated like a pampered pet. They enjoy the outward display of affection. They feel appreciated, prized, valued. It is a boost to their self-esteem. To those who did not receive a lot of affection in their formative years, it is a big boost." He smiled. "Again, your prejudices are showing. If you are to enter this world and find Lady Annabelle, you must understand and accept their mindset." He paused, his fingers steepled. "Or should I inform Her Majesty that you have declined the assignment?"

Damn the man. He knew she would never do anything to displease the Queen. "Of course not, I am honored that she requested my assistance."

"Then read the invitation in your hands. It is imperative

that you attend."

Tillie opened the envelope and read the card within. "Annual Husbandry Auction, the twenty-ninth of June, please provide code upon acceptance. *L'Academie des Paturages Humains.*" Her face screwed up in puzzlement. "Quite secretive. No time. No place. No means of response. If this fell into the wrong hands, they would simply toss it."

"Indeed. Regular participants know they are to meet at a pre-designated spot for transport, after the dinner hour. You will receive the exact time when making your reservation because if you do not know how to make the reservation, you are not one of their own."

"Am I to go into this lion's den alone?"

"Not at all. Agent Ali will accompany you. Some aspects of the auction may be offensive to a woman of your discerning tastes." He attempted to squelch his grin, but his blue-gray eyes filled with amusement. "Security is tight there. If you display any discomfort at what you see, things could get dicey. You may be removed from the premises or worse."

Tillie waved her hand at her superior. "I've seen women's breasts before. Why would that concern me?"

The man cleared his throat. His face flushed. "They aren't breasts, they are *teats*, and they need to be physically examined to ensure that they have not been damaged in the milking process. Human cows must also be checked in other orifices for damage and disease. Also, they must be assessed for personality, temperament, breeding, and milk production. It is very technical. They are treated like animals, not humans. To do otherwise would expose you as a fraud. We are told the price of a human cow is based on their animalistic qualities. There may also be a few bulls in the auction, men responsible for breeding the Hucows. They must be similarly examined."

Tillie's face reddened. Suddenly, she felt quite queasy. She started to speak, but her superior held up his hand.

"There's more. This is a human-animal auction. It is not limited to Hucows. There will be Hupigs, Huhorses, and maybe even, Husheep. Fortunately, you are to focus on the cows. That is where we believe Lady Annabelle will be found."

Tillie gazed at him. "What if she isn't there? What if she has changed . . . er, species?"

"I suggest you cross that bridge when you come to it."

"And what am I to do if I find Lady Annabelle? How do I extract her?"

"You purchase her at the auction. You have been given sufficient funds to bid up to one million Euros."

Tillie's eyes grew wide. "Criminy. That much?"

Lord Ryder nodded. "These cows are well-trained and well-treated. The females are pampered — weekly manicures, hair treatments, and such. A happy cow is a happy milker, as they say."

Tillie's eyes widened. "Lady Annabelle *could* be there willingly? She is not necessarily a captive, forced be a Hucow?"

"Exactly. And that is our dilemma. While the Queen hopes that she is there willingly, several factors are at play. Lady Annabelle may have freely joined a farm to become a Hucow, or she may just have danced on the wild side and somehow wound up at auction. In the alternative, she may have been kidnapped and forced to become a Hucow, or she may have been forced and now enjoys the lifestyle. There are all sorts of reasons she could be there and all sorts of reasons she prefers to stay. Our only mission is to get her out."

Tillie frowned. "Why would they put her up for auction? Isn't that a way to get rid of unproductive or uncooperative cows?"

"Not necessarily. Some farms simply raise and train Hucows, then sell them. Given their going rate, it is a lucrative business. A great way to supplement the income from a regular farm. Human cows bring much more *lucre* than actual farm-raised cows."

Tillie sighed. "For just one day, I would like to forget that there are a whole lot of people engaged in activities that far surpass my imagination."

Lord Ryder's mouth curved up into a wry smile. "Then we would be out of a job."

Tillie tapped her jaw, considering. "You know, this might be a better job for the Yanks. They are a kinky bunch. I believe there was a recent study that found them to be the kinkiest country in the world."

Lord Ryder snorted. "If you were the Queen, would you want that bunch of kinksters to know your relatives are participating in like behavior? Why, their intelligence services would find a way to use it against us for decades." He shook his head. "No. This we do alone."

CHAPTER TWO: THE AUCTION

"Honey, I'm home."

Tillie sat up from the sofa and rubbed her eyes. While waiting for her lover and roommate to return from his assignment in Morocco, she had fallen asleep—with visions of women with drooping teats pirouetting through her head.

Abdul Ali swept into the room and pulled her into his arms, his kiss deep and passionate. "Tillie, my love, I missed you." He growled. "I couldn't wait to get out of there." His brown eyes gazed at her lovingly and his tender smile lit up his handsome, aristocratic face.

An Arab prince with joint British and Saudi Arabian citizenship and a fellow MISix agent, Abdul had been assigned as her mentor when she first entered the service. It did not take him long to work his way into her bed, then into her heart. During their last assignment together, he had declared his intentions, and after months of ardent pursuit, she had capitulated. It hadn't been difficult. Tillie did enjoy his company, and between the sheets, he was the creative sort. He was a bit cheeky at times, but that was part of his charm. Tillie was thankful his position as a barrister had proved to be without challenge, compelling him to join MISix. Otherwise, their paths would never have crossed.

She smiled up at him. "Well, I imagine without Prince Mustapha to act as your pimp, things were quite a bore." She giggled. "What a surprise."

He laughed and nuzzled her neck. "*Au contraire*, my dear. The Prince may be dead and gone, but his business thrives.

One of his lieutenants stepped in before they could clean up the, er, his remains."

Tillie could not hide her disgust. "Someone else is trafficking women and men? Stealing them off the street or otherwise luring them in?"

Abdul shrugged. "You know how they operate. Traffickers just regroup and hide under a new rock. If it is any comfort, they are no longer pursuing blonde, blue-eyed women such as yourself. This time, they seem to be trafficking people from the Pacific Rim." He tugged on a lock of Tillie's hair and pulled her close. "I may enjoy the occasional scene with restraints, a flogger, and some nipple clamps, maybe even a few drops of candle wax, but those customers are hardened sadists. Whips, chains, stretchers, crosses, suspension, and outrageous toys are common, as are gang bangs and other sordid activities. They have devised ways to torture all orifices, and I mean extreme torture." He reached under her shirt and palmed her breast, then pinched a nipple. "They get off on pain. They enjoy screams. And they prefer their victims lose consciousness."

Tillie squeaked and pulled away from him, rubbing the abused breast. "Dammit, I hate it when you do that."

He grabbed her again and planted his mouth on her nipple. "Exactly," he cooed.

Tillie grabbed his thick dark hair and pushed him away. "And how would you classify people who engage in pet play?"

Abdul smirked. "For a long time, I thought it was a way to avoid a desire for bestiality. If you cannot stomach fucking, or being fucked, by an animal, why not substitute the animal for someone pretending to be one? There is a sheikh I know who has a whole harem of Hucows in his palace. You walk into this lavishly furnished room with women who have grotesque teats draped over chaise loungers or curled up on the floor. Some are clothed, some are not. They are bathed, massaged, or otherwise groomed, all the while mooing in delight.

"He claims to milk them so he can feed the younger children within his care, but he and his minions seem to delight in sampling *the goods*. Not just their milk, but all of their holes. I don't get the fascination with fucking a human who has been mutilated and deformed. I try to be tolerant, but that seems inhumane."

Tillie snuggled up to him. Abdul really was a handsome man. Tall, pleasingly fit, and incredibly handsome. His light brown skin only added to his allure. At times, it was difficult not to touch him. She ran a hand over his broad chest. "I've been thinking about that. They create their own Frankensteins, with a twist. They are playing God and in effect, creating monsters."

Abdul ran a finger along her thigh. *"You are my creator, but I am your master."*

Tillie stared at him. "What?"

Abdul grinned. "It's a line from that movie, *Frankenstein*. In the end, the monster turns against his creator and kills him, for the act of creating him."

Tillie shuddered. She pointed at her chest. "If anyone hooked me up to a milking machine and turned these into udders, I would be apoplectic. I *would* seek revenge."

"Which is why anyone forced to be a Hucow is probably there willingly or sedated. Either doped up or addicted to drugs. One thing I noticed about the Hucows I observed was that they were quite subdued. Very docile. I was sure they had been drugged." He shrugged. "That wouldn't be very healthy for others drinking their milk." He shrugged. "I don't know. Maybe they were hypnotized or brainwashed."

Tillie scowled. "Mind control, or some form of psychological manipulation? I hate that. How can someone do that to another human being?"

Abdul studied her. "How is that any different than a

wealthy man who requires his trophy wife to submit to multiple surgeries to transform her face and body in a way that pleases him? It's just as dehumanizing." He took her hands and peered into her eyes. "We have to face facts, darling. There are a lot of perverse people out there. All we can do is try to prevent them from doing significant harm." Abdul pulled her in for another kiss. "Enough about work, my little vixen. Time for bed, and I mean bed. I would never ask you to sleep on the floor, in a cage."

Tillie laughed. "As if."

After being picked up at a car park in central London, Tillie and Abdul were blindfolded for the duration of the trip. When they arrived at their destination, the blindfolds were removed and they were offered partial face masks, the kind typically worn to masquerade balls. Not surprisingly, the masks matched their elegant evening clothes — her expensive designer gown and his craftily tailored tuxedo.

Tillie gazed at Abdul. His mask depicted an enraged devil. Hers was more feminine, more refined. Tillie imagined she would appear almost faceless, much like the masks worn in some cults. "Well, I guess these will have to do. I know who you are, but you won't be recognized by anyone else."

Abdul chuckled. "On the other hand, you, my dear, can hide your beautiful face, but your blonde hair and luscious body are dead giveaways. Thank God the mask has that thick netting over the eyes. Those blue eyes of yours are very distinctive."

The town car pulled up to a well-lit barn. "Why is the barn painted red?" Tillie muttered. "Why not green or blue?" She shifted, nervous.

"I suppose that is more an indication of the origins of the owner than anything else. Americans paint their barns red. It is a tradition started by the early colonists. I believe they created some sort of red sealant to protect the wood used to erect a barn. Here, so many of the barns were constructed with stone, so if painted at all, it tends to be with white paint."

Tillie snickered. "Aren't you the historian? Who knew?"

Abdul chuckled. "I did learn *something* in those British boarding schools I was forced to attend."

Tillie smiled. "Ah, yes. You led a very privileged life as a child, as I recall."

Abdul rolled his eyes. "And I am very grateful my father had the funds to ship us there. It was that or roaming the desert for the rest of my life. Life in the Middle East has come a long way in recent years, but when I was a child, things were fairly primitive. The wealthiest families had tutors, of course, but my father saw the benefits of establishing relationships with the British, thank Allah."

The chauffeur opened the door of the car and Abdul exited. He turned to assist Tillie. They walked on a red carpet into the barn. The crowd was well-dressed and extremely high-spirited. Tillie was sure that if she sniffed the air, she would smell money. Lots and lots of money.

"Be careful, darling," Abdul murmured "Your disdain is showing. You need to play nice with the locals. Plaster that sweet smile on your face."

Tillie gazed at the large gathering. It could easily be one of the many high society soirees she was often required to attend. Everyone was dressed in expensive designer attire, and the women were heavily laden with jewels and other expensive fripperies. A large bar was set up along one wall. Two formally attired barmen were frantically mixing cocktails, while waiters served champagne and canapes. It was hard to believe this was the setting for an auction of human cows.

She forced a smile and said sweetly, "Let's grab a catalog and have a look around, shall we?" Tillie took Abdul's arm and held on tightly. She didn't know the qualifications for a

Hucow, but she didn't want to find herself on the wrong end of a milker.

Abdul chuckled. "Perhaps you would feel better with a collar and leash, my dear."

"And get mistaken for an animal? Not on your life." She tugged on his arm. "Let's get this over with."

They exited the room through a large door manned by security and entered another large barn the length of a British football pitch and just as wide. It was divided into sections, each with an overhanging sign. Cows. Bulls. Pigs. Horses. Pets. Underneath each sign was a multitude of stalls and cages. Even more startling, the creatures being shown were mooing, squealing, neighing, meowing, and yipping. Tillie felt physically ill. There were hundreds of humans on display, altered either physically or with protheses to resemble animals. It was grotesque.

Abdul nuzzled her neck and whispered, "Good God, Tillie. You are white as a ghost." He pulled her into an embrace. "Are you feeling faint?"

Tillie took a few deep breaths. She had to do this. No matter how profane, she had a job to do. She tried to clear her mind, to unsee the horror of so many disfigured people. *Don't see, don't think, just do, Tillie.* She pulled out of Abdul's embrace. "I can do this. I can."

Abdul nodded and led her to the section labeled *cows*. Most of them were lying on straw pallets or standing at the fences, watching the crowd. A few were set off from the others, lying on sofas in poses not unlike pin-up girls. The signage affixed to the stalls was labeled *Graded*. The area with the sofas bore a sign that said *Pedigreed*.

Tillie gazed at Abdul. "This is confusing. Pedigreed? Graded?"

Abdul clucked his tongue. "You are such a city girl, darling. Pedigreed cows have a well-documented lineage and

milking record. They are the aristocrats. They are mostly
those with some royal blood. Graded cows are the lower clas-
ses. Not necessarily well-bred, but satisfactory milk produc-
ers. Think upstairs—downstairs. Not all Hucows are created
equal." He pulled her toward the pedigreed stall. "The pedigreed cows are much more expensive and typically offer
higher quality milk, as well as preferred genetics for breeding."

Tillie was sure she was about to be pushed beyond the
threshold of ridiculousness into pure horror. But she remained silent. She would keep her eyes peeled for Lady Annabelle and ignore the rest of it. There were ten cows in the
Pedigreed enclosure. They were in various states of disfigure-
ment. All had large teats. Some were bound in slings, while
others were hanging free. One woman bore the markings of a
Holstein, others resembled Brown Swiss or Guernsey cows.
Some faces had been altered to appear more cow-like, with
broad noses, large mouths, and plump lips. Several had tails
that actually twitched. It was difficult to tell if the cow markings were make-up, tattoos, or something else, but they were
done professionally.

"No gaping, Tillie," Abdul muttered. "You are supposed
to be admiring their beauty." He nodded at the stable hand
and said in a commanding voice, "I should like to inspect the
Holstein and that Guernsey." He pointed. "The one with the
graceful ears."

Tillie held back a snort. *Graceful ears?* What the bloody hell?

The stable hand entered the pen and spoke to the Holstein,
gently helping her onto her feet. Hunched over, but not on all
fours, the cow walked stiffly to the fence. Though encased in
a harness, her huge teats swung awkwardly as she walked. It
was obvious they interfered with her mobility. Her boots,
made to resemble hooves, further hobbled her. The stable
hand attached a leash to her collar and then to the fence, and

stepped back. He slapped her on her flank and said, "Now be a good cow, Harriet."

The cow possessed large eyes and a strangely deformed jaw. Her lips were plump and red. Her snout was petite, but a large gold ring hung from her nostrils, stretching them grotesquely. Up close, it was clear that her hair had once been blonde, but was now dyed black. She even wore gloves designed to look like hooves.

Abdul entered the enclosure and walked around the cow, his expression intent. He pointed to a brand on the cow's backside. "Has she been registered?"

The stable hand nodded. "All of our pedigree cows have been officially registered, sir."

Tillie studied Harriet. Her face was almost cartoonish. In addition to the plump red lips, the cow's blue eyes appeared to have been tattooed with eyeliner and somehow were framed with long thick lashes. Tillie found Harriet's expression troubling. It was difficult to determine whether she was happy or sad. Her eyes were simply vacant.

Abdul gently took the cow's head in his hands and opened her mouth. While she had some teeth on the bottom—all widely spaced apart—there were no teeth on the top, only pink gum. Just like a real cow. "Has her mouth been trained?"

Tillie tried to hide her disgust. *Trained for what?*

The stable hand patted the cow's backside. "She is one of the best suckers we have, sir. We have had no complaints. As you know, without upper teeth, she cannot bite, so that makes her mouth extra pleasurable. You are welcome to sample her . . ."

The cow's lips suckled Abdul's hand and he chuckled. "That won't be necessary. She is clearly quite capable of pleasing a man's appendages." He reached into his pocket and removed what appeared to be a dog treat. He laid it on the palm of his hand and offered it to the cow. A delicate pink tongue shot through her lips and scooped it up. The cow chewed, then swallowed. She mooed softly and again nuzzled Abdul.

Tillie blinked. The Hucow's jaw moved as if she was chewing cud. Tillie inhaled, slowly. Thank God Abdul was taking the lead. She was so out of her element.

Abdul asked, "Has she been bred?"

"No, sir."

Abdul removed her teats from the harness and inspected each with his hands. "And how is her milk production? Her teats are quite large. I am concerned that she may have been over milked."

The stable hand smiled. "Harriet is quite fond of the milker, sir. In fact, she has progressed from the goat milker to a standard bovine machine. She is happiest when producing milk, so we tend to indulge her. We stop when she indicates she is done." He grabbed one of the teats and compressed the nipple. Milk sprayed out. "Would you like a taste, sir?"

Abdul nodded and pressed the other nipple. Again, a stream of milk sprayed out, and Abdul stuck a finger in it, then licked his finger. He raised his eyebrows in surprise. "Quite sweet and very rich. High quality. I assume she can be milked by a human as well? By suckling?"

The stable hand's face reddened. "Yes, sir."

Tillie fought back an insult. *Dirty little twat.* From the way the stable hand was touching Harriet, it was obvious he was well familiar with her assets. She glared at the young man but remained silent.

Abdul squatted and ran his hands over her legs. "Any problems with bearing the weight of her teats? How have her legs handled the added stress from the weight gain?"

"She is adjusting well, sir. Her legs were quite strong when she was brought to us. She has been exercised regularly to build up strength."

Abdul extended a hand. "Her records, please?"

The stable hand handed a clipboard to Abdul. "As you can see, she is disease-free. We test our stock weekly."

Abdul took the board and stood behind the Hucow. "I assume she is on a diet of heavy fiber to ensure a healthy digestive system?"

"Quite healthy, sir. She poops twice a day, on schedule."

"And what of her tail?"

"Anal plug, only, sir. Since that is a matter of personal preference, we left that to her potential purchaser."

Abdul stood. "Please roll her on her side so I can check her genitals."

The Hucow was rolled onto her side, exposing a puffy, enlarged pussy. It had been stripped of all hair.

Abdul frowned. "I thought no attempt had been made to breed her."

The stable-hand again flushed. "All sexual contact has been voluntary, and usually, initiated by the cow herself. I'm afraid this one finds the milking process arousing. She often finishes her milking sessions with a good old-fashioned fucking. Of course, she has also had access to a variety of sexual aids to prepare her for breeding. The Sybian is one of her favorites. That's a saddle with a dildo attached that she —"

"I know what it is," Abdul growled.

The man nodded stiffly. "Anyway, she was quite tight when acquired and it was felt that some stretching was in order. Of course, safety measures were strictly enforced."

Abdul stared at the man. His mouth twitched. His hand flexed. Tillie was sure he was going to pounce and beat the man into unconsciousness. Instead, he smiled politely and said, "Then I will insist she be tested again before final payment. The last thing I need is an infected cow passing an STD to my herd."

The man paled. He stuttered, "Of course, sir. Absolutely. We would never sell a diseased cow . . ."

"I hope not." Abdul made a note on the auction catalog and nodded at the brown and white Guernsey. The cow moved up him and nuzzled his body, very close to his cock.

Tillie giggled.

Abdul frowned. "What amuses you so, darling?"

Tillie blushed. "It's just that she seems so . . . um . . . friendly."

The cow swung her head toward Tillie. Angry brown eyes gazed at her. Although there was a fence between them, Tillie took a step back. Unlike the other cow, this one still had some life in her. She was still fighting. The Guernsey's face was untouched, except for a large ring in her nose and a bit in her mouth. Her teats were smaller than the Holstein and hung free. Her hair appeared to be a natural brown.

"This one's transition appears to be incomplete," Tillie said. "How long has she been with you?"

"Only two months, but the stablemaster felt she might do better with a hands-on owner, someone who can devote more time to her training." He patted the cow's head. "Millicent came to us naturally brown, so her hide has been altered to make her markings more distinct. Except for her nose and mouth, there were really no other necessary alterations." He motioned toward her vagina. "There has been some misbehavior. She does not play well with others, so we thought it best to transfer her to a permanent owner."

The cow glared at the stable hand. Then she swung her head toward Abdul and nuzzled his cock.

Abdul patted her head. "She is rather friendly. I am drawn to her temperament. After my inspection, I would like to peruse her papers as well."

Abdul went on to inspect three graded cows and continued to make notes in his catalog. He only requested the paperwork on one.

Tillie's respect for his operational skills grew. Obviously, Abdul had studied up on dairy cows and understood the factors important to real buyers. As they left the pen, Tillie whispered, "I don't see anyone who resembles Lady Annabelle. Has this been a total waste?"

"Actually, I want to inspect both pedigreed cows further," Abdul said. "Millicent seemed to know me. Not sure if that means anything, but she may be of use. The other one reminds me of someone, possibly a person I observed on a missing person's posting. I think we need to take both with us. And one of the cows in the graded pen is on my list as well. She's related to royalty, so I am surprised she was not put with the pedigreed stock. Maybe her production has been substandard,"

Tillie muttered, "They look like something you'd see in a freak show. Going home will be difficult, especially emotionally. I only hope some of the disfigurements can be reversed."

"*If* they want them reversed. Remember, darling. Some of these women are here voluntarily. They wished to become a Hucow. To you, it may be degrading and humiliating, but some may enjoy being degraded. They may find it empowering. You can't discount that. Nor can we treat anyone as a victim, until we can confirm that is what they actually are."

He led her to the pen labeled *Bulls*. Tillie was unable to stop her mouth from dropping open. Seven men, all wearing loin cloths, roamed around the enclosure. Despite the coverings, it was obvious that each was *well-hung*. Abnormally so. "Crickey, they look like the stars of a bad porn movie," she whispered.

"And that is probably where most will wind up unless someone desires them for penetration or breeding purposes. All of their genitals were probably chemically or surgically enhanced. And their fertility, either naturally or chemically, is off the charts. In addition to serving Hucows, they may also be purchased by women or men for sex or breeding."

Tillie scrunched her nose. "Like a gigolo? That's obscene."

Abdul laughed. "Sometimes, I forget how sheltered you are. In my culture, I have seen everything. It is not uncommon for a sheikh with erectile dysfunction to hire such a bull to impregnate his harem. Multiple pregnancies are a sign of great virility. No one knows how those children were sired except for the sheikh and the women."

"Those poor women," Tillie moaned. "That must feel like they are being impaled on a baseball bat."

"As you know, what the woman feels is often irrelevant. A sheikh gets what a sheikh wants."

Tillie stopped and stared into the distance. She nudged Abdul. "What the hell are those people doing? Look at them. That's inhumane." She pointed at a cage filled with a variety of human animals. The sign overhead proclaimed it was a *petting zoo*, but people were doing more than petting. They were poking and prodding with a variety of instruments, laughing with delight at the Hu-animals' response. Some squealed, others cowered. A few peed themselves. Others simply collapsed on the ground and curled up into a ball. The alleged buyers seemed to have no qualms about abusing them.

"Careful, my dear." Abdul took her hand. "We're guests here, not a judge and jury. It is not our place to interfere." He sighed. "This is why Ryder sent me along. At this point, you would have your badge out, trying to shut the place down. You have to remember. We have one mission and one mission only. Find and extract Lady Annabelle. We haven't found her yet. We need to keep looking." He ushered her away from the petting zoo and walked through the area designated for Hu-swine. He placed his arm around Tillie and nuzzled her neck. "Remember, hide your revulsion. You are supposed to be curious. Fascinated, even."

Tillie bit her lip as they toured the pig pens. These humans were distinguished by their obesity. Again, most were female, and all were nude. The sows lay lazily in the pens, their bodies on full display. Some had long flowing hair with fabric pig ears, nose adornments, and heavily made-up eyes. Others had faces that more closely resembled pigs, with snouts, jowls, very short hair, and surgically enhanced ears. Most had hands covered with gloves that resembled cow fingers and their feet were in boots that looked like hind pig feet. Pig tails were obviously an important feature. They were evident in all shapes, sizes, and colors. Tillie assumed they were butt plugs, but really, who knew unless they were inspected? In the middle of the pen was a mud puddle and several of the sows were rolling in it, squealing with delight. *An animal mud-wrestling match.*

The boars were more muscular. Large incisors protruded from their mouths. While their genitalia did not appear to be enhanced, it was well-developed. Several of the sows were flirting with the boars by rubbing against them or offering their hind ends.

Abdul pointed at a female being mounted by a male pig or boar. "Never underestimate a sow in heat. Any boar will do."

Tillie flushed. "That is just so . . . so primal."

"Exactly." He pointed at one of the sows She was young and not as heavy as the others. "That one wears a crown. I wonder if it is for adornment or a reflection of her breeding." He beckoned a stable hand and pointed at the piglet. "May I see her papers, please?"

Tillie studied her. "Do you think she's a royal?"

"Possibly. Bloodlines are just as important with hogs as any other species. There are so many breeds, but some are superior and claim a much higher price."

Tillie leaned into Abdul. "I am so glad you're with me. There is no way I could have learned all this in a fortnight."

Abdul kissed her. "Don't discount the danger of an unaccompanied female agent in this type of setting." He turned to the approaching stable hand, who handed him a tablet.

"It's all there, sir," the man said.

Abdul studied it. Then he gazed at the stable hand. "Has all of this information been verified?"

The stable hand nodded. "Oh, yes, sir. We verified it."

Abdul handed the tablet back to the man, then pulled the catalog from his pocket and made a note. "Thank you," he said to the man. "You've been very helpful." He gently tugged at Tillie and moved away from the hog pens.

"Well?"

"Eastern European with ties to the Austro-Hungarian Empire. No political power, but good bloodlines. A princess without a kingdom."

Tillie sighed. "And we don't know if she's here voluntarily or a captive."

Abdul shrugged. "When it comes to human trafficking, anything is possible. You know that. Where there is demand, there is always someone willing to fulfill it. That is just the way it is. Now let's check out the stable. I want to make sure Lady Annabelle did not wind up there."

A loud bell sounded and the lights dimmed. "Dammit," Abdul muttered. "I really need to check the horses."

A man dressed in a suit stopped next to him and smiled. "Our stables were open for viewing only. We will not be selling any ponies today." He gestured toward a grilled cage, similar to the cash-out booths in a casino. "Please register for the auction. It will begin in thirty minutes."

Tillie and Abdul were led to a cashier's counter. A woman took Abdul's false passport and black card and scanned them with a handheld computer. She smiled when something popped up on the screen. She pointed to another set of doors. "Thank you for participating in our twenty-fifth annual husbandry auction." Then she turned to the next participant.

Abdul's arm went around Tillie's waist and he guided her

through the doors. "Come on, let's get a seat in front. I don't want to miss a thing."

The auction was held in another large barn. Although it smelled like hay, none was in evidence. The place had been swept clean. Instead, there was a stage with a podium and sound equipment. A tall man wearing a cowboy hat stood off to the side, chatting with a woman and a stable hand. He appeared to be all cowboy, with boots, spurs, jeans, a checked flannel shirt, and bolo tie. The man was also romance-novel handsome, with a chiseled face, deep tan, and piercing blue eyes. His Rolex watch and a large diamond ring on a middle finger hinted at his wealth.

As the man spoke, the woman blushed and giggled. Even the stable hand appeared enthralled. Tillie wasn't surprised. A successful auctioneer required quick wit and an engaging personality. The man appeared to be a perfect fit.

Tillie and Abdul settled into elegant armchairs in the front row. She focused on the people entering by the side door. People of all ethnicities flowed into the room. Men in tuxedos were followed by men in thaubs—the robes men often wore in the Middle East. Women in glittering cocktail dresses bedecked with jewels mingled with women in business suits, saris, and hijabs. Their wealth was obvious, not only from the quality of their clothing, but from their posture. These people were accustomed to the best of the best.

Tillie leaned toward Abdul and whispered, "Do you recognize anyone? I have some guesses, but with those masks, that's all I have . . . guesses."

Abdul adjusted his bow tie. "Not to worry. I am feeding all of this to Smythe. We will have their identities before we arrive back at the drop-off point."

Tillie smiled and kissed his cheek. "Now why didn't I think of that?" She tapped her tiny purse. "There wasn't time to insert a tiny camera in here, but with your video, we should have it covered."

Abdul's grin was wicked. "At least we're using this video for the good of the Crown. I seem to recall the misuse of another camera on our last assignment, you dirty girl."

Tillie playfully slapped at his arm. "Just a small souvenir, in case you forget how to entertain me in your old age." She winked. "God knows, you are ten years older than me. Your mind is bound to deteriorate long before mine."

He nuzzled her neck. "You have benefited from every year of my superior experience."

The crowd began to head toward the chairs. Each collected a paddle laid out on the seats. Suddenly, the excited voices that had been bouncing off the aluminum walls calmed.

Tillie fiddled with her paddle. She took a few deep breaths. The lights dimmed and a spotlight was focused on the podium. The man with the cowboy hat entered the light and grinned at the bidders. It was clear he thought the situation amusing.

"Well, hi ya'all, welcome to this here auction." The man's drawl was low and slow and seemed to boom from the rafters. It was also indisputably American. "I'm Jay and I'm your auctioneer this evening. Remember, this is a fundraiser, for *L'Academie des Paturages Humains*." The audience tittered at his perfect French. He grinned. "Whaaat? You thought a Texas cowboy couldn't speak French?" He leaned forward as if to take the audience into his confidence. His expression was sly. "That's what you get when your grandpaw hooks up with a sweet Parisian lady during the Great War. Sometimes, I think we imported half the single women in Paris to Texas after we marched down the *Avenue des Champs-Elysees*."

His comments were rewarded with laughter. Some people clapped.

"Alright, folks. Let's get busy. You have your catalogs and you've had time to inspect the herds. But we're gonna shake things up a bit. We're gonna start with the premium lots." He chuckled. "Prime American beef, if you will. They aren't listed in the catalog because this shipment was delayed by some pesky border agents. But that situation's been resolved and they arrived this afternoon. And I'm tellin' ya, they are some hot properties. I suspect you're gonna be emptying your wallets tonight." He winked at his audience. "And remember, this is a fundraiser, so be generous. Shoot, some of you can probably get a tax write-off."

Tillie gazed at Abdul and cocked an eyebrow. Prime *American* beef? Did that mean Lady Annabelle was not among them?

Abdul patted her leg and placed an arm around her shoulders. "Just let it play out. Besides, American beef *is* prime. None of these people would eat domestic beef. It is too stringy."

Tillie huffed, but she settled her head onto his shoulder, ensuring that everyone around them saw nothing but a happy couple.

Jay looked stage right and nodded at someone behind the curtain. "The first item up for auction is a lovely pair of heifers. Sisters, originally from the great state of North Carolina in the United States. They're offered to you today by a cattle-rancher from the great state of Montana."

A male tender led two females onto the stage by a leash. They appeared to be identical. Each had long, white-blonde hair, large blue eyes, and pink, full lips. Their teats were thin and elongated but hovered above the floor. They wore cowbells around their necks and cow tails in their arses. Without those *enhancements*, they would have been quite beautiful. The tender gently pushed them onto their knees and the young women fell onto all fours.

Tillie tried not to wince. The girls appeared quite uncomfortable. How did they get here? Were they here willingly?

Did they truly want to be auctioned off, or did they want to go home? She knew so little about what was going on in the heads of these people. Tillie sighed. While the auction gave every appearance of being real, what if it was just a bit of theatre? Some sort of performance, rather than reality? It was not unusual for wealthy people to have some strange sexual peccadilloes. And they clearly were not above enjoying the humiliation of others. Their behavior in the petting zoo had proven that. Maybe this type of theatre appealed to them. Maybe they enjoyed debasing the underclasses.

Jay continued, "Now these cows could use some fattening up, but they're young yet. Plenty of room to grow." He smirked. "Neither has born a calf, but both have been certified fertile. Since they are so new to the farm, only a little reconstruction has occurred. They have been on the goat milker for just two months, but their production continues to increase. Currently, they are naturally producing roughly 10 liters or 2.5 gallons a day. However, with the use of Domperidone, that output could easily increase to 20 liters. Thus far, their milk has received a five-cow rating. Sweet and fatty."

Tillie watched the women's faces carefully. One of them flinched when fertility was mentioned. The other paled. In unison, they lifted their heads and gazed directly at Tillie. Their eyes were filled with confusion. And fear. Tillie *saw* fear. Those two were not in this auction willingly. She would bet they were being trafficked. They required rescue.

The cows looked at each other, their eyes glistening. Abdul shifted in his chair and frowned.

Tillie squeezed his hand. *Good. He sees it, too. If he doesn't bid on them, I will. I may not be able to save everyone, but I can save these two. Then the Yanks will owe me one.*

"If you will turn on the tablets the attendants are distributing, all further information on Lula-Bell and Clara-Bell is in File One," Jay said. He stooped down and said something to the women, then slapped each on their flanks. The women wiggled their asses and mooed. Jay grabbed Lula-Bell's teat and squeezed the nipple. A burst of fluid shot out. He licked a finger and nodded. He did the same to Clara-Bell. Then he stood up and said, "Some of the sweetest milk, I've ever tasted. Definitely five cows." The five-cow rating was primarily used in the United States and given only to high-quality milking cows.

He gazed out at the crowd. "These two were definitely worth waiting for." He cupped a hand around his mouth as if telling a secret. "And Clara-bell is a virgin." His grin was crooked. "Now, remember, to accommodate our diverse audience, trading will be done in Euros, not U.S. dollars or British pounds. Currency converters are available on your tablets. Let's begin the bidding at two hundred thousand Euros."

Tillie leaned over to Abdul and whispered, "What's my limit?"

Abdul gazed at her. "You have no limit. You have no budget. I am to do the bidding. I am the only one with a limit or lack thereof."

Tillie gave him the stink-eye. "And why is that?"

"Because this crowd is filled with misogynists. You will notice that no other women are bidding. If you want to call attention to yourself, just raise that paddle."

Tillie huffed. "Then you bid and you win. They are not here willingly."

Abdul nodded and lifted his paddle.

The bids stopped at one million Euros. Jay slammed down his gavel and pointed at Abdul. "Sold! To this fine gentleman and his beautiful companion. Please see the cashier."

Abdul bowed his head, rose, and quickly left the room.

The two women gazed at Tillie. She was at a loss at how to respond. Finally, she allowed a slight smile and nodded at the two women. At least she could give them hope.

Abdul returned to his seat and the next auction item was

introduced. A large dark-skinned man with long dreadlocks sauntered onto the stage. He had an extremely large cock and horns on his head. He grinned at the crowd and waggled his eyebrows. His crooked grin and bright eyes made his amusement clear. His gaze swept the room, then landed on Tillie. His grin widened, revealing bright white teeth. He winked.

What the hell? Tillie stared at him. He was certainly handsome, but unfamiliar. She was sure they had never met. Why had he winked at her? Was he trying to convey a message or was he merely flirting?

"That bull seems to be taken with you," Abdul whispered as he slid back into his chair. "Should I bid on him?"

Tillie shook her head. "I'm not sure. He acts as if he knows me, but I think he's just flirting. And he is too comfortable up there. Let him be. I suspect he is here willingly." She tried not to smirk. "I also think he enjoys his work."

Abdul smiled at her. "What's not to enjoy? He breeds Hucows. His only job is to impregnate women." He chuckled. "Maybe he thinks you are a prostitute, a comrade in arms."

Tillie rolled her eyes. "Thanks for that. Maybe I should bid on him just to annoy you."

Abdul snorted. "Please, you already have a bull in your bed. You do not need another."

Tillie giggled. "And will you wear horns, too? They are quite attractive."

Abdul kissed her cheek and growled, "Only if you'll wear kitten ears and a nice fluffy tail,"

Jay stepped up to the podium. "Well, this here is one of our prize bulls, folks. What we call a prime breeder. His bloodlines are superior. He comes from a long line of large and muscular bulls, many of whom are tribal chiefs in remote parts of Africa. He has been in service just a year and already has twenty calves to his credit, all healthy and strong. While the owner is selling the bull, he retains rights to his semen. All negotiable, of course."

A swarthy man with dark hair and eyes waved a hand at the auctioneer. "Why is he being sold? He appears to be prime stock."

Jay smiled. "His owner is getting out of the business. He no longer has any need for a full-time bull. Now if you will look at your tablets, the paperwork on the bull is in File Two. Take a look at the photos of his calves. Those are some beautiful babies."

Tillie's eyes rounded. Why would anyone agree to be sold, especially when they were not in receipt of the profits?

Jay crooned, "Now let's begin the bidding at two hundred fifty-thousand Euros."

CHAPTER THREE: A MERE GLIMPSE

More lots followed and the bidding continued for over an hour. The auctioneer offered five alleged Hucows for auction. Most were sold for around a million Euros.

Tillie impatiently tapped her knee with her fingers. Only one lot was left. She prayed it was Lady Annabelle.

"And finally, we have a world-class cow for ya'll, folks." Jay grinned. "Her bloodlines are pure, royal on both sides. Prime breeding and or milking stock. Check her stats in File Ten. They are truly amazing. And she's young, so she has many years of breeding ahead. She is rated five-plus cows. Her milk is creamy and sweet. A top seller." He nodded at someone behind the stage and a female cow was led out by the tender.

Tillie gasped and Abdul quickly grabbed her hand. Lady Annabelle. She barely resembled the photos that had been supplied. The former Lady Annabelle had been lithe and blonde. An English rose. Her face had resembled a pixie—large green eyes, a button nose, creamy complexion, and rose-bud lips.

The Hucow before them appeared to have been horribly mutilated. Her teats were exceptionally swollen and were barely contained in a harness. While her eyes were still green, they were framed with almost comically long, dark lashes. Her nose was significantly larger than in the photos. A septum piercing with a large chunk of metal stretched her nostrils. Her lips were large and pillowy, as if injected with enormous amounts of some kind of filler. A thick metal collar, from which a jeweled cowbell dangled, encased her neck.

Although Lady Annabelle had retained her blonde hair, it was now braided and wrapped around her head, bringing attention to her ears, which no longer resembled a human's. They were now large flaps. The jeweled crown affixed to her head added a humorous element to her appearance. Lady Annabelle's feet appeared deformed, altered to resemble cloven hooves. Her hands were gloved and also mimicked a cow's hoof.

"Oh, my." Tillie gazed at Abdul. "I didn't expect this." She nodded at Lady Annabelle. "Do you think her pussy has been surgically altered? It looks a cow's udder. Surely, they haven't—"

"I am hoping that is some sort of prosthesis." Abdul winced. "If all of that has been done against her will, she has a very long road to recovery ahead of her."

"Well folks, this is one of our best-pedigreed cows." Jay walked over to Lady Annabelle and pinched her rump. She mooed. He chuckled and grinned at the crowd. "She has been extensively altered to ensure that her body suits her new role. Ain't she beautiful?"

The audiences applauded vigorously. Some even whistled.

Tillie felt ill. Even if they managed to rescue Lady Annabelle, she doubted all of the *enhancements* made could be reversed. The royal would spend the rest of her life disfigured, probably hidden from the world. She studied Lady Annabelle's eyes. Like so many of the others, she revealed no emotion. Was she drugged or broken? While Tillie doubted any human could survive that type of mutilation, she restrained her thinking. They still didn't know if Lady Annabelle's transformation was voluntary or coerced. Tillie didn't want to believe that anyone would willingly be disfigured, but she had seen a lot of strange things in her career. The answers she needed would come only after Lady Annabelle was interviewed. Tillie placed her hand on Abdul's chest and leaned into him. "Do we really want to rescue her? She's been subjected to some atrocious mutilation. What if they can't correct her deformities? What if she has to remain like that her entire life?"

"That's not our decision to make." Abdul's tone was irritated. "I'm sure the Queen will throw all of her resources behind her recovery. However, it is not the physical deformities that worry me. It's the psychological ones. Think of the horror of being subjected to that sort of mutilation. How does one survive *that*?"

"I'm glad that answer is not ours to give. I imagine she will be put under suicide watch for the rest of her life."

Jay pounded his gavel. "Okay, so let's begin the bidding on this Jewel of the Crown at one million Euros."

Tillie could barely hide her horror as paddle after paddle went up into the air. When the bids approached two million Euros, she shoved her paddle in the air and gazed at Jay. She continued to hold her paddle up, indicating she would top any other bid.

"Tillie, what the hell are you doing?" Abdul whispered. He put his paddle back on his knee, as did several others. He glared at her.

"Saving a woman's life," she muttered.

"Looks like Annabelle has a few admirers," Jay crowed. He nodded at someone as the bid increased.

Tillie turned and examined the remaining bidder. Her face reddened as she recognized the man. Anders Mark, her sometime nemesis and lead operative with The Agency. His mask did little to hide his piercing green eyes and his classic smirk. Besides, his tuxedo did not disguise his well-muscled physique, a dead giveaway to those who knew him. She muttered, "What are the bloody Yanks doing here?"

Abdul groaned and turned. He glared at Anders.

35

An expression of surprise flitted across Anders' face, then he nodded as if conceding, and put his paddle down.

Anders Mark was the head of a team of undercover agents who operated off the books in the United States. The secretive organization had morphed into a covert arm of the Executive Branch, sent out only on missions beyond the reach and authority of traditional intelligence services.

Tillie had crossed paths with Anders' team on several occasions, unintentionally interfering with their missions. Eventually, the Americans had sought retribution and Tillie narrowly escaped termination. To appease the Americans, MISix had agreed to provide her services to The Agency upon request. Tillie had participated in one successful mission — the illegal imprisonment scheme — but had not heard from The Agency since. She had no idea what Anders was doing at this particular auction. He could be on a mission to rescue an American citizen or to gather evidence on one of the auction participants. She found it strange that they had both been bidding on Lady Annabelle, though. Were their missions once again related?

Tillie sighed. *Dammit*. When the Yanks were involved, her arse was the one that wound up on the whipping bench. Hopefully, this time they would stay out of her way.

"Sold! To the pretty lady in the first row!" Jay slammed down his gavel. The audience applauded and Tillie bowed her head in acknowledgment. "Please pay the cashier."

Tillie grabbed Abdul's hand and they rose. As they made their way to the cashier, Jay announced, "As you know, all other bids must be submitted on your tablet. The entire catalog appears in File Eleven. Initial bids are due in thirty minutes. You'll have another fifteen minutes for follow-up bids and then final bids will be due in one hour. Those not interested in bidding may proceed to the reception area, where your transportation will be waiting. On behalf of the

L'Academie des Paturages Humains, I thank you for your participation in this evening's event and your generosity. I hope to see you back next year." He smiled and turned away from the podium. He said something to Lady Annabelle, but she slowly shook her head. The cow's expression became mournful and she turned her head away from the auctioneer.

About two-thirds of the participants stood and moved to the exit doors. Tillie narrowed her eyes. "None of those people bid at the auction?"

Abdul shrugged. "I imagine some just come for the show. Maybe they have a strange fascination with Hu-beasts but would never purchase one. You know how the wealthy are. Easily bored. Desperate for entertainment."

"What do you think Agent Mark is doing here? And why was he bidding on Lady Annabelle?"

Abdul shrugged, apparently unconcerned. "Perhaps the Americans have a few pedigree cows of their own in this auction. Maybe they were trying to deflect from their true interest. The auctioneer is American. Maybe he is their target. Hucows, in particular, are rumored to be big business in the western United States. Some ranchers see it as a secondary line of income. Some farm them for their own purposes, others supply pimps and slave traffickers, and still others supply the porn industry."

They arrived at the cashier, and Abdul handed over his black card. The cashier asked, "And how do you wish to transport your purchases this evening, sir?"

"When I am done bidding, I shall arrange for private transportation, but I will collect all of the necessary paperwork at the end of the evening."

The woman handed him his black card and a receipt. "Very good, sir."

At that moment, a loud air horn sounded. Tillie turned swiftly and looked for its source.

The cashier muttered, "Blimey, the peelers," and ducked down behind her cage.

Uniformed police and men in suits stormed into the room, guns drawn. Abdul sighed. "Just go with it, darling. We will get things straightened out later. First, we need to figure out who's in charge."

Tillie's gaze landed on Anders Mark, who was speaking to a man in a dark suit and gesturing toward the stage. "Let's hope it's not the damn Yanks."

Tillie and Abdul were cuffed by a stern, efficient constable and led to a motorcoach. Anders — his mask still on — emerged from the crowd and spoke with the officer. The man grunted and handed Anders a key. Then he walked away.

Anders smiled at Tillie and Abdul and gestured toward a police car. "This way, folks."

Tillie glared at him and opened her mouth to speak.

Anders tapped her arm and muttered, "Not here. Too many unfriendly ears."

"But we—"

Abdul cleared his throat. "Not now, *dear*."

Anders led them to the car and ushered them into the back seat, then slipped into the front passenger side.

Tillie ripped off her mask and exploded. "What the bloody hell, Anders? If you blew our operation, I am going to string you up by your balls." Tillie slapped at the seat. "You are lucky I am wearing cuffs. Otherwise, you would be bleeding all over this car."

The female driver, attired in a blue suit and hat, turned and grinned at Tillie. "Aw, give the man a break. We didn't know the Brits were involved. We thought it was merely on offshore auction held by some Texans."

Tillie gasped. "Dianna? I thought you were stateside popping out babies or something."

Dianna rolled her eyes. "Just because I had a child or two doesn't mean I lost my brains. However, technically, I am along for the ride. After we sort this mess out, Anders and I are headed for a week in London, then Paris. The kiddos are with Mom and Dad on the farm in Wisconsin."

Abdul chuckled. "Should I expect to see my niece flitting around somewhere?" He removed his mask and grinned.

Abdul's niece, Hope Ali, was a member of The Agency and on Anders' team.

Anders shook his head. "The rest of the team is working the shipping side, in the States. We're just here to identify the Americans involved and track the victim's new owners so we can make arrests and retrievals." He removed his mask and wiped the sweat from his brow with a monogrammed hand-kerchief. "Did you see that last woman? My God, she's been totally mutilated. I expected the large teats for milking. I did not anticipate some of the other grotesque transformations."

"That is one of ours," Tillie said. "We were sent by the Queen to retrieve her. Why were you bidding on her?"

Anders shrugged. "For leverage, in case I needed someone to trade for more Americans. I also needed to bid on someone who wasn't an American. I didn't want to make anyone suspicious. As it was, I barely managed to get into the auction. I knew I was under suspicion. So why not bid for the grand prize?"

"We need to get her back." Tillie's tone was insistent. "We can't afford to lose her."

Anders took out his phone. "Do you have a name?"

"Annabelle. Lady Annabelle Travers."

Anders pushed a few buttons and brought the phone to his ear. "This is Agent Mark. At tonight's auction, there was a Hucow. Lady Annabelle Travers. She was the last one on the stage. The one with blonde hair and all sorts of other altera-tions. I need her held for pickup by MISix." Anders listened, then nodded. "Let me know when you have her secured."

He disconnected. "They'll let me know when she's ready for release. They're in the process of sorting through the victims, trying to get IDs. Some of those people can no longer speak. I don't know if they're actually mute, are out of practice, or are being obstinate. And if they don't have any identification with them, we are in a right pickle."

Dianna snorted. "A right pickle? As opposed to a wrong one? Sorry, he's been hanging around with too many farmers."

Anders nudged her. "Says the farmer's daughter." He ran a hand over his face and shuddered. "God, I have seen some horrible things, but that was above and beyond. It was surreal."

Dianna patted his arm. "A lot of what we do isn't pretty, hon. We did manage to prevent most of them from being sold, and that's what's important." She peered in the rearview mirror at Tillie. "One of these days, we're going to get an assignment that doesn't involve human trafficking. You get kidnapped once by a slave cartel, and everyone thinks you're an expert." She grinned at Tillie.

When Dianna was in her early twenties, she and Tillie had been kidnapped by the same slave trafficking organization, one that specialized in young, blue-eyed blondes. When they bonded in captivity, Dianna was still in law school, and Tillie had just joined MISix, working undercover. Their next encounter occurred after Dianna joined The Agency and both were investigating a cult leader, Reverend John of God's Delight. The reverend lured college kids to his Peruvian compound and used them as slave labor. When the cult leader showed an interest in Dianna, Tillie spiked her coffee with herbs that would make her sick and thereby avoid a sexual assault by Reverend John. Unfortunately, Tillie miscalculated. Dianna grew horribly sick and almost died. While they had made amends, they remained a bit wary of each other. Still, Dianna's demeanor was now friendly.

Tillie felt a wave of relief. Beings at odds with Dianna had unsettled her. As an MISix agent, she didn't have many friends, but she would have liked to count Dianna as one of them. Tillie chuckled. "Maybe you should join MISix. Our royals get in all kinds of trouble. I get some sweet assignments. Monte Carlo, Mykonos, Belize, all over the world. The only trafficking cases I have worked on were with you Yanks. The rest of my cases involve blackmail, gigolos, theft, and drugs."

Anders grinned. "We do the dirty work so you can have fun." He gazed at Abdul. "What's up with you two, anyway? I thought you'd be married by now."

Abdul held out his manacled hands. "How am I supposed to propose when I've been shackled?"

Anders flinched and withdrew a key from his pocket. "Sorry about that. Tillie in handcuffs is such a welcome sight, given her predilection for interfering with our assignments." He chuckled and unlocked Abdul's restraints. He handed Abdul the key. "In case you want to play later."

Abdul laughed. He took the key and unlocked Tillie's cuffs. He placed the cuffs and key in his pocket. "I *will* hang onto to these. Having an extra set never hurts."

Anders smirked. "I always knew you Brits were closet kinksters." His phone rang and he swiped the screen. "Agent Mark." His eyes darted to Abdul and Tillie. "I understand. Get someone to look into it, see if there are any leads. Someone must have seen something. And grab the security footage, if there is any." He disconnected and gazed at Tillie. "We have a problem."

Tillie tilted her head. "Which is?"

"Lady Annabelle is missing."

Tillie scowled. "How the hell did that happen? I thought

the authorities had that place locked down. Besides, the poor woman could barely walk, after what was done to her feet. She had to have had help. Or she was taken. Kidnapped." She glared at Anders. "I knew I should have taken her into custody right away."

Abdul patted her leg, and she brushed him off. He gazed at her. "Except, we were undercover, dear. If you expose your cover, you also expose mine. I cannot allow that. Neither of us would be able to work in the field again. And I, for one, do not wish to spend the rest of my career attached to a desk."

Dianna slowed the car and pulled off the roadway. She turned toward the back seat. "He's right, you know. And since we took you two into custody, you could blow our covers as well." A stern expression crossed her face. "That's not a risk I'm willing to take. If you want to go back, you go alone and at least try to wear some sort of disguise." Dianna growled. "I don't know why I'm surprised. You almost blew my cover once and then you almost got me killed. Your recklessness is a hazard for anyone who works with you. I expect better from MISix."

So much for Dianna's friendly demeanor. Tillie gasped. "I would never intentionally — "

"You put others at risk without a second thought." Anders eyes narrowed. "Which is why you are still indebted to the United States for your actions." He nodded at Abdul. "She almost got your niece, Hope, killed. Remember that?" He snorted, obviously disgusted. "If I had my way, your credentials would have been revoked for that. Dammit, Tillie. Did you learn nothing from your recklessness?"

Tillie's face reddened. She was surprised to feel tears rush to her eyes. In a defensive voice, she replied, "Then what do you suggest I do? My assignment was to find and retrieve Lady Annabelle. I found and lost her. What now?"

Anders closed his eyes and took a deep breath. "You allow

Interpol to investigate, see if they have any leads. Then you allow Dianna, who if you remember, is a world-class hacker, to search the Dark Web and elsewhere to try to track her. As much as I hate to say this, we will work with you. To protect our covers. But I swear to God, Tillie, if you fuck up this time, I will ask my president to call the Queen and demand your beheading. What we do is too important to have some two-bit spy mess it up."

Tillie swiped at her tears and pursed her lips. "That's harsh and very unnecessary."

Dianna cocked an eyebrow. "I certainly hope so. I thought we had gotten past all that. I thought we were building toward a more cordial relationship. Prove it. Let's keep things on that track, shall we?"

CHAPTER FOUR: SEARCHING... AND SEARCHING

The four agents immediately drove to Tillie and Abdul's townhouse. While the MISix agents changed into more comfortable clothing, Dianna and Anders set up a command center, with a laptop computer, a white board, and phones.

When Tillie entered the sitting room, Dianna turned the computer screen toward her. "Do you know any of these people?"

Tillie squinted at the information. "Not personally, but Jay Abernathy was the auctioneer."

Dianna nodded. "Well, we know he trains Hucows. He even boards some of them. We've found his ads for training on all the major fetish sites. That part of his operation appears to be legal. Just a bunch of people who have fantasies about being cows. We've been unable to find any evidence that he is trafficking his trainees, but we haven't been able to get close enough to verify that. It's not like these people make trips into town so we can question them, and legally, we have no right to conduct a search of his farms. We need probable cause that a crime has been committed. We were hoping to get something at the auction, but the raid — which we did not instigate, by the way — threw a wrench into things. We still don't have any answers."

Tillie frowned. "The Yanks were not behind the raid? But I thought..."

Dianna shook her head. "Definitely not us. We planned to

44

buy some of the Americans on auction and get some answers. Heck, we don't even know if Hucows are real or some sort of fantasy thing, or if people were actually being sold. Hucows could be a smoke and mirrors thing. An illusion created by people skilled in makeup and costuming. Think about it, someone made a lot of money off of the people you bid on. When the raid occurred, the sellers got to keep the money, and they didn't have to deliver the people purchased."

"It was all a scam?"

Dianna sighed. "It could have been a fundraiser. Kind of sick, if you ask me, but an effective way to raise funds for the *L'Academie des Paturages Humains*. The money from those sales did arrive in their bank account, but it could just be a funnel, a place to wash illegal funds. All we can do now is watch where the money ultimately lands."

"So, you have no evidence that Abernathy has done anything illegal?"

Dianna scowled. "Nope. And as far as I can tell, his only link to Lady Annabelle is that he might have trained her and she boarded one of his trucks." Dianna called up surveillance footage from the auction site and pointed. "There she is, walking up the ramp. No one is forcing her."

"What does that mean?"

"I have no idea. Abernathy Farms is an international farming conglomerate. It owns farms throughout Europe and the United States. They raise livestock — dairy cows, beef steers, swine. Their Hucow training program seems almost frivolous. They don't need the money. What we don't know is whether the program is for shits and grins, or a more serious, money-making pursuit. Sure, they had some of their *trainees* up for auction, but that may be part of the whole gig. In the BDSM world, some women crave being auctioned off as slaves. Maybe this is simply an extension of that.

"If these people aren't being trafficked, if everything *is* consensual, we really have nothing to hang them on." Tillie closed her eyes, her face scrunched up in concentration. Then she sat up straight and her eyes flew open. "What about the sale of their milk? From the look of those women's teats, they have been pushed to the extreme to produce milk. That can't be voluntary."

Dianna shook her head. "There's nothing illegal about selling breast milk. Women do it all the time. I'm not even sure why it's being sold on the black market unless the buyers don't want to be known. And now, there is evidence that breast milk has all sorts of benefits, even for adults, so the demand is even greater. Selling humans is illegal, but selling Hucow milk is not. As long as it isn't regulated, we can't even get them on selling tainted milk. God knows they have to be using some sort of drug to increase production. Unless we can get them on forced labor or trafficking charges, we have nothing." Her expression sobered. "Believe it or not, there seem to be some women who want to be milk slaves or milkmaids, as some preferred to be called. That's why they become Hucows."

Tillie frowned. "However, most of the people for sale at that auction seemed unbearably sad. And there were hundreds more hu-animals in the other barn. I can't believe that many people would . . ."

"Yet, no one seemed to object to the auction, did they? Wouldn't the auction be the perfect opportunity to expose their objections? Hell, if it was me and I was there unwillingly, I would make it known."

Tillie narrowed her eyes. "Unless they were drugged or otherwise forced into silence."

Dianna turned back to the computer screen and stared at the information it held. She shrugged. "Tillie, unless we can interview some of those people, we will have no idea what was going on. The best we can do is investigate the backgrounds of those sold—but not really sold—and see if any of them have been reported missing. At this point, I wouldn't be surprised if they were all actors."

"But their teats," Tillie screeched. "What women in her right mind would permit her breasts to be mutilated into some grotesque version of a . . . a gigantic banger? Surely they did not submit to that willingly."

Dianna emitted a long, drawn-out sigh. "I can't believe I have to remind you of God's Delight. The people in that cult were lured in and became forced labor. They were subjected to long days in the blistering hot sun, bugs, everything we consider unpleasant. Yet, when we raided their compound and gave them a chance to leave, many stayed. I think we need to accept that some people have needs we will never understand. Some need to be followers, some need to be humiliated, some need to live in a fantasy world. Just because we find their behavior repugnant does not mean it's wrong. Even if we can prove aggressive, even abusive, milking practices, as long as there is informed consent, we've got nothing."

Tillie's shoulders slumped in defeat. "Okay. I get that, but it doesn't help me with my biggest problem. How do I find Lady Annabelle?"

Dianna studied Tillie. Hesitantly, she offered, "Well, being a Hucow is considered a sexual fetish in several different ways, not just because of the milk production, but for the bedroom games. Maybe Lady Annabelle prefers to be treated like a cow in the bedroom. Or maybe she is seeking attention from a man who has a Hucow fantasy." Gently, Dianna added, "Or, maybe, she wants to be a porn star for the fetish industry."

Tillie gasped but said nothing. She studied her hands, seemingly lost in thought. Then her gaze returned to Dianna. "If she is a Hucow willingly, I guess her motives are not important, are they? All that matters is her rescue or retrieval. So how do I find her then?"

Dianna offered a slight smile. "Let me play around on the Dark Web. If she is on there for any reason, we'll have a place to start. I did input the information from her records at the auction. Let's see if that leads to anything." Dianna turned back to her computer and typed in a few commands. The screen blinked and shifted as it searched. Slowly, information filled the screen. A profile of Lady Annabelle appeared, accompanied by two photos—one as an unaltered woman and the other after she had been molded into a cow. Dianna's eyebrows shot up. "Wow, she was quite pretty. It's a shame to have—

Tillie's eyes narrowed. "Why is all of that information on the Dark Web?"

Dianna studied the profile, then made a few more keystrokes. She frowned. "Apparently she's up for sale. Not only for sale but discounted for a quick sale. Someone wants to unload her fast."

"Who is selling her?"

Dianna searched the profile and shook her head. "That's strange. No seller is listed." She turned to Tillie. "Either whoever is selling her wants to distance themselves from the transaction or she is selling herself."

Tillie groaned. "Can we bid on her?"

Dianna typed in a few more commands. "I think I can break into the bidding system, but I need to list a funding account. I assume MISix has one?"

Tillie nodded. "They gave us a black card for bidding. What's the top bid right now?"

Dianna studied the screen. "It looks like two hundred thousand U.S."

"It shifted from euros to dollars? Interesting. Does that mean she has been transported to America, or that whoever has her is American?"

"Not necessarily. Let me check the shipping costs." Dianna typed in a command and raised an eyebrow. "Wow, maybe she *has* been transported overseas or at least is headed there. The shipping charge is extreme."

"Instead of shipping, can she be picked up?"

Dianna reviewed the profile page and clicked on a button. "Blind pickup for U.S. citizens only. That would indicate she was or will be stateside."

"Blind pickup?"

"They send you a receipt with instructions for pickup at a freight warehouse, usually not affiliated with the seller. The warehouse is simply used to store freight of a certain size."

Tillie sighed. "So American involvement is unavoidable. Damn."

Dianna smirked. "Hey, we're trying to help, here. Besides, you need us if she is on American soil. A Brit snooping around an American farm is sure to raise eyebrows." She turned back to the screen. "But first, we need to win the auction." She hit a button labeled *bid*. "This setup is the same as most auction sites. You can authorize automatically increased bids if someone outbids you. The only difference is, they also accept Bitcoin, which can cloak the funding source. Dollars are easier to track." She turned back to Tillie. "What do you want to do?"

Tillie hesitated, then handed her a plain black credit card. "I swiped this from Abdul. He said it had a limit of ten million U.S. dollars. Let's increase the bid in increments of five thousand dollars. And try to identify the other bidders. "

Dianna entered the information, and almost immediately a warning popped up on the screen. "It says we've already been outbid. Someone has initiated the automatic bidding system. We may have a long night ahead of us. Bidding ends at midnight and hundreds of bids could come in at the last minute. If we want to outbid everyone else, I'm going to need to break into the system and rig it in our favor."

"You can do that?"

Dianna nodded. She stretched and yawned. "Un-huh, but I'm going to need coffee, lots and lots of coffee."

Tillie grinned. "Sorry, all I've got is tea."

Dianna's eyes narrowed. "Then I suggest you order up some coffee. Americans dumped all that tea in Boston Harbor for a reason." She screwed up her face. "That stuff is disgusting."

Tillie was exhausted.

It had taken Dianna over an hour to break into the auction site bidding system and rig it in their favor. Once Abdul and Anders arrived with coffee and pastries, Dianna had become more animated and energized. In addition to monitoring the bids, she had checked in on her baby girls, twice, cooing over FaceTime and then handing it off to Anders, who sang some nonsensical lullaby. Tillie thought it amusing that such hard-core secret agents could be so soft when it came to babies.

Abdul nudged her. "That's you and I in a few years."

Tillie snorted. "First, you have to convince me to marry you. Then you have to convince me to breed." She shook her head. "Sorry, not in my plans. I want to be carted out of MISix after dying at my desk. I have no plans to exchange sleuthing for nappies."

Abdul nuzzled her. "You will change your mind. I can be very persuasive." He nipped her ear, and Tillie pushed him away. Abdul chuckled. "You may be a bit ornery, but all that stubbornness will melt away after I've put a baby in your belly."

Anders laughed. "Would you two like to be left alone? Dianna and I can always move to our hotel."

Tillie shot him a stink-eye. "We are here to work." She slapped at Abdul's chest. "Behave. We have work to do."

A loud blaring noise filled the room. Dianna grabbed her phone and blushed. "Sorry, baby feeding time. I have to pump . . ." She blushed again and pointed at Anders. "Keep an eye on the auction." Then she grabbed her purse and left the room.

Abdul arched an eyebrow. "I don't think I want to know what that was about."

Anders laughed. "Just wait, bucko. You're going to learn about all sorts of things you never wanted to know." He sat in Dianna's chair and peered at the computer. "There's an hour left in the auction, but we're still the high bidder." He frowned at the screen. "Wow, the numbers are getting up there. The bids are almost up to a million dollars. Someone wants Lady Annabelle bad. Good thing we've got the upper hand. Otherwise, Lady Annabelle might slip away."

Tillie moved to the computer. "Can you pull up the names of the bidders?"

Anders shook his head. "All are code names, but Dianna has been extracting their Internet Protocol addresses to find them." He started typing. "She's already set up a separate file so after she's done . . . uh . . . milking . . ." He flushed.

Abdul grinned. "All perfectly natural, mate. No reason to be embarrassed. It is easy to forget that a woman's breasts serve an important purpose, especially when they are affixed to nipple chains and rigged up with rope." His gaze went to Tillie's breasts and he grinned. "Then they are beautiful. Just beautiful."

Tillie blushed and turned away. *Damn that man. He just doesn't know when to turn it off.* It was hard enough for a woman to be taken seriously at MISix. When your work partner was also your life partner, the lines got blurred, and Abdul was not shy about crossing them.

She studied the screen. "My word, the bidding is fairly constant."

Anders nodded. "A new bid every few minutes now. On some auction sites, you can set up to bid at the very last minute from multiple computers. That helps block out competitors. But sometimes, you wind up bidding against yourself." He grinned. "Wasted money, but that doesn't matter if you win."

Tillie gazed at him. "What on earth would you be bidding on? You don't strike me as the online auction type."

Anders shrugged. "I'm trying to find all the great comics my grandfather gave to me. My mother gave them away. The Incredible Hulk. Spiderman. X-men. Some of the early Star Wars."

Tillie studied him. "That must cost a bloody fortune."

Anders nodded. "But every time I get a new one, I visit my grandfather and we read them together. Gives us both a break from our routines. It still kills me that my mom simply delivered them to Goodwill. Someone got *very* lucky." He gazed at Tillie. "Didn't you collect anything as a child? Something that still brings good memories?"

Softly, Tillie said, "Teacups."

Anders laughed, loudly. "Did you say *teacups*? That's so, so *feminine*."

Tillie's arched her spine and hissed, "What exactly are you implying? I'm not feminine?"

Abdul stood, his expression fierce. "Answer carefully, mate. It appears you have insulted *my woman*."

Anders held up his hands. "Woah, it wasn't meant as an insult. It's just that collecting teacups seems so dainty. I simply can't imagine Tillie as a child at a tea party, you know, in a gingham dress and big hair bow. She such a—"

Tillie kicked Anders, and he winced. Then he pointed at her. "There. That's exactly what I'm talking about. I picture her getting into brawls with the boys, kicking, spitting, and scratching." He struggled not to grin. "Not playing with *teacups."*

Dianna came back into the room. "Teacups? What about teacups?" Her gaze moved from Anders to Tillie.

"*Kickass* Tillie collects *teacups.*"

Dianna giggled. "So what? They're pretty. Just because she was a tomboy doesn't mean she doesn't appreciate pretty things. I collected porcelain cows. That doesn't mean I was a farm girl, always in overalls and work boots."

Anders stared at her. "But you *did* grow up on a farm."

Dianna waved him off. "By the time I was ten, my mom had me on the road with beauty pageants. I spent most of my childhood primped and pampered. I wouldn't have dared to get my hands dirty playing with the cows. And my dad wouldn't have permitted me to milk one. That was my brother's job."

Tillie smiled. "I think your husband has a little problem with assumptions. As you Americans like to say, *when you assume, you make an ass out of you and me.*"

Anders ran a hand through his long brown hair. "Crap. I walked right into that."

Abdul grinned. "Indeed."

The computer beeped and all eyes turned toward the screen. Dianna pushed Anders out of her chair and peered at the screen. "Holy cow, she's running up some big numbers. I can't believe so many are bidding." Dianna frowned. "Her milk production numbers aren't that great, so they intend to use her for other purposes." She switched screens. "I recognize some of these bidders. Almost all of them are involved in slave trafficking, as buyers and sellers."

"So, they plan to prostitute her?"

"Maybe. Some of these people run fetish farms or bordellos, but a few pornographers are bidding as well." She searched the list of bidders. "And a guy who specializes in snuff films." Snuff films were usually graphic and violent, ending in a murder.

Tillie gasped. "Why would they want her?"

Anders cleared his throat. "Those guys subject their victims to horrendous things. They abuse and torture them until they plead for death. I can't even imagine how those guys would play with Lady Annabelle, especially with her . . . uh, alterations." His face paled and he shuddered. "God, where my mind just went." He paused for a moment, then continued. "Since she's a royal, they would torture her as long as possible, probably even live stream it on the Dark Web. There are a lot of sickos out there. They'd clammer to watch it. They might also use her for extortion. *Pay us or we will execute her,* that sort of thing."

"That would kill the Queen." Tillie tried to hold back tears.

Abdul put his arms around Tillie and pulled her against him. "And after extorting money, they will probably wind up killing her anyway. Murdering a royal would be great publicity and pleasing, in certain quarters." He gazed at Anders. "Is Marwolaeth I'r Frenhines among the bidders."

Tillie stiffened. "Death to the Monarchy? How the hell did we get from human farming to sex trafficking to terrorist groups?"

Dianna shook her head. "Ah, the wonders of the Dark Web. The one place where you can find everything you need, even when you're not looking. I'll check on The Mars when the auction is over. Those people are opportunists, and they aren't about to pass up an opportunity to harm the Queen." She squinted at the screen, her fatigue apparent. "Five minutes to go."

CHAPTER FIVE: WINNING ISN'T EVERY-THING

They won the auction for Lady Annabelle, barely. Anders turned off his phone and frowned. "The number I was given to arrange for pickup has been disconnected."

Dianna sighed. "And the auction has been expunged from the Dark Web. It appears Lady Annabelle's owners have taken a powder, with Lady Annabelle in tow." She gazed at Tillie. "Did they withdraw any funds from your Black Card?"

Tillie nodded. "The full amount. They got their money. Almost two million U.S. dollars. Why take a runner?"

Anders shrugged. "We had no guarantee they would deliver Lady Annabelle. Hell, they might not even have her. It could all have been a scam. It's not like we can run to the police and report this. We're not dealing with upstanding citizens here. They *are* criminals." He nudged his wife. "At least Dianna can get your money back."

Tillie buried her head in her hands. "What am I to tell Her Majesty?"

"Nothing, yet," Anders said. "Let's have some of my people check out Abernathy Farms in the U.S. Maybe we can find her and snatch her back on our own. Unfortunately, given the nature of the other bidders, I'm pretty sure we're not the only ones looking for her, and that worries me. Especially with The Mars back in the picture. We narrowly beat out their bid."

Several years prior, The Mars, short for Marwolaeth I'r Frenhines or Death to the Monarchy, hijacked a plane with several high-profile Americans on board. They had used Chinese technology to cloak the plane, making it invisible to radar and other tracking systems. Eventually, the plane was buried in a Wisconsin cornfield, the passengers still alive and in their seats. Dianna and Anders had been among those who rescued them, shortly before The Mars blew up the plane.

Dianna gazed at him. "I thought most of The Mars were still at Guantanamo."

Anders shook his head. "Apparently, some of them have been released. The *minor players*." He sighed. "When will we learn that with terrorists, there are no minor players. Everyone has the potential to become the next Bin Laden. What I want to know is where they got their money. We bankrupted them. They must have a new backer."

"Which makes them dangerous, again." Dianna shook her head sadly. "On the plus side, we know what they look like. We can pick them out in a crowd. On the negative side, they know what we look like. We won't be of much help there. We're better off finding Abernathy and taking it from there." She gazed at Tillie. "But this is your case. We don't need to be involved. It's totally up to you." She grabbed Ander's hand. "I am perfectly happy heading out for my second honeymoon."

Tillie steepled her fingers. "This *is* my assignment. I am authorized to do whatever it takes to bring it to a successful conclusion. However, as you can imagine, this is a rather sensitive mission. If word of this leaks out, it could have a serious impact on the Monarchy. So, the fewer people involved the better."

Abdul nodded. "Personally, I don't want to elevate this to a joint mission. However, we could use some help with finding Jay Abernathy, especially if he has debunked over the pond. Maybe you could alert passport control, and if he crosses your border, you could arrange for someone to track him and find out if he still has Lady Annabelle. If she isn't in evidence, we will need assistance in setting up an interrogation."

Dianna tapped on her keyboard, then pointed at her screen. "I put in a search request for all ships and trucking concerns owned or leased by Abernathy Farms. It looks like they own two livestock carriers and a trucking company in the UK. We need to know if one of their ships left port in the past few days and where it's headed. Their trucks are monitored by satellite, so that's the easy part. I already broke into their computers and got the codes."

Abdul raised an eyebrow.

Dianna chuckled. "What? I was bored and struggling to stay awake. I had to do something. Abernathy was on my list, so I just went with it."

Tillie grinned. "Are you sure you don't want to join MISix? I could use someone like you."

Dianna shook her head. "Sorry. Once a Yank, always a Yank."

Abdul rolled his eyes. "What about private planes? Shipping by sea takes up to seven, maybe eight days. Since the Hucows are technically human, a private plane would be much faster and probably safer. We're talking hours rather than days. Plus, the planes could land at a private airport anywhere. That would be easier than shipping and transporting by truck." He gestured at Dianna's computer. "Check for planes and private or corporate airstrips. Abernathy strikes me as the type to travel in style."

Dianna's fingers flew across the keyboard. She waited a minute, then typed some more. Finally, she said, "An Airbus A330, registered to Abernathy Farms, departed Cardiff late last evening. The flight plan lists the destination as Logan for refueling only, then on to a private airstrip near Dallas. It is scheduled to land at Logan in about an hour." She gazed at

Anders. "Is it too late to get Customs involved? If we can get someone to board the plane when it lands and conduct an inspection, this could be wrapped up quickly. Customs can put a hold on the cargo until Tillie can get there and seize it. *If Lady Annabelle is aboard.*"

Abdul pulled at his dark goatee. "We'll need to get our documents in order as well."

Tillie held up a hand, "Let's not put all of our eggs in one basket. We don't know if Lady Annabelle is on that freight plane. As you said, we don't even know if she has been taken. Dianna, please check the area docks for ships and Abernathy farms for truck traffic. My gut tells me she's still here. It would be too risky to transport her overseas. Whatever plan is underway, she is of more value in the U.K."

Dianna typed in a few commands and waited. She smiled. "Good call. No ships, but several trucks are headed to two different farms, one in Manchester, the other in York." She spun around in her chair. "Your call, Tillie."

Tillie gazed at Abdul, her eyebrow raised in question. "What do you think?"

He straightened up in his chair. "I think we can cover Cardiff and the farms, but we're going to need help in the states. Maybe the plane could be searched by your customs service at Logan, then tracked to Dallas. We have no idea who is on board or where they are taking them. We might need that information."

Dianna keyed in a few more commands. She waited a minute and keyed in a few more. She turned off the laptop and stood. "All set on our end."

Tillie's eyes narrowed. "That was fast."

Dianna waved her off. "You forget, we do this sort of thing all the time. Our team has been activated already. Some of our agents are on their way to Dallas, and we'll have satellite surveillance set up by the time Abernathy lands at Logan. We will have to jump through a few hoops, warrants and such, but it's all doable." She smiled at Anders. "Which means our second honeymoon is still on."

Anders grinned. "Then, let's get a move on." He grabbed Dianna's hand. "I'm sure you two can handle it from here." He nodded at Abdul. "Your niece, Hope, is on point. She'll be in touch after the Customs search at Logan."

Tillie groaned. "Great. Not my biggest fan. If anything, she will go out of her way to embarrass me."

Anders shrugged. "Doesn't change the fact that she's one of the best agents we've got. If she doesn't find anything, you can be confident there is nothing to be found, at least in the states. She's got our file and the photos. Once she gets over the shock of what was done to Lady Annabelle, she'll be good to go."

Dianna winced. "I almost feel sorry for Jay Abernathy. He's going to be lucky if he gets out of this with his balls attached. We call Hope *castrator-in-chief*. She doesn't play nice with men who hurt women."

Abdul shook his head and chuckled. "Trust me, she comes by that anger honestly. My brother and his wife chase down terrorists and sue them for victim compensation, putting their own lives at risk. Hope has a very strong sense of humanity, and of right and wrong. If she finds any Hucows, Abernathy will be the recipient of her fury."

"Well, if you're lucky, you'll find Lady Annabelle here." Dianna tugged at Ander's hand. "Now, we've got ninety-six hours with no interruptions. I intend to enjoy it. See you on the flipside." She started moving toward the door, then stopped and went back for her computer. "Almost forgot that this is mine. I sent you the file."

Tillie watched them hustle out the door. "Guess we need to get busy, then."

Abdul grinned.

Tillie swatted his head. "With the case." She sighed dramatically. "We don't have time for *that*."

Tillie pulled her truck off the road near the Manchester Abernathy Farm and turned off the engine. She gazed at the four members of her team, all dressed in black, with night vision goggles hanging around their necks. "We're going to have to walk the rest of the way. I want to make sure they don't see us until we launch our raid. Remember, shoot only if they shoot first. Tasers or body darts first, then bullets. I want to keep as many of them alive as possible."

"What about the animals — I mean hu-animals — I mean victims?" The agent blushed, then tugged at his goggles, his frustration apparent. "I am afraid I don't know what to call them."

Tillie sighed. "No matter what has occurred, no matter what has been done to them, they are still human. They are victims until we learn otherwise. They should be treated with respect and addressed as ma'am or sir."

The agent nodded. "What I meant to ask was are the hu-animals likely to give us any problems?"

Tillie checked her tranquilizer gun. "No idea. If any of them get unruly, tranq them. Ideally, we can get most of them out of there before our presence is discovered. I want to avoid alerting security or the owners if possible." She pulled her goggles over her eyes and waved at her team. "Let's go." She paused. "Keep your eyes open for mines, trip wires, and other types of surveillance. This place is bound to be fully wired."

They picked their way through the thickly forested perimeter, scaled a four-foot fence, and danced around a few land mines, clearly set out in the open to deter intruders, not animals. Finally, Tillie's team arrived at the farm. There were three large barns, a well-fenced-in pasture, and a large, two-story farmhouse. The barnyard was well-lit.

"Damn," Tillie muttered. She pulled off her night vision

goggles. "Those lights are going to make a stealthy approach difficult." She tapped on her earpiece. "Team Two? Any visuals?"

Her com crackled. "Team Two in place." Abdul's voice was soft but clear. "They've got eyes everywhere. No way are we going to get anyone out of there without alerting them."

"What if we cut the power?"

"Too noticeable."

"Do we even know if someone is in the house?"

"The lights are turning off and on at random as if the residents are present."

"Could be timers."

"My guess would be humans. Someone has to take care of the herds."

Tillie peered at the house. Lights *were* blinking off and on, but there were no shadows indicating the presence of people. "Get someone up close to look in the windows."

"On it."

Tillie motioned to her team to fall back and wait. After a few minutes, her com crackled.

Abdul said, "No people on the first floor. No way we can scale the house to check the second floor without being detected."

Tillie gazed at the house again. "Either they are sleeping or that house is empty. All the lights on the first floor are now off. However, if they are asleep, they need to be subdued. Even if it is empty, someone may be monitoring from afar."

"What do you want to do?"

"Get two in the house on the first floor to search and subdue, if necessary. If the house is empty, I say take out the power and haul arse before anyone notices. We do a quick search and if Lady Annabelle isn't here, we decamp. If there are any humans in those barns, we can send in the clean-up crew after we leave. I don't want to alert anyone if she isn't here. They might move her before we can catch up."

"Maybe we should regroup, hit both farms at the same time."

Tillie pursed her lips. "If she is here, I don't want to lose her."

"Stop and think, Agent Spencer. Is it worth endangering the lives of so many for one particular victim, even if she is royal?" Abdul's voice grew stern. "As I recall, this is why we got our wrists slapped last time. We have no room for impulsive behavior."

Tillie's snapped, "But what if someone else shows up and snatches her? What if the terrorists or traffickers get in here before we can make our move? If we delay, we not only lose the element of surprise, we risk losing her altogether."

"At least get a team in place at the other farm. Hedge our bets."

Tillie frowned. "How long will that take?"

"A few hours, tops. Meanwhile, we've got the perimeter secured."

"So, we just sit and wait?"

Abdul sighed. "Unless we can figure out a way to get into those barns without being seen."

"I'm going in."

"Agent Spencer . . ."

"Hear me out. I'm small, and if I stick to the ground, they will think I'm an animal. I'm dressed all in black, and in the shadows, I will be hard to see."

"At least wait until the other team is on their way to the other farm."

Tillie sighed. "Okay, call it in. I will wait an hour, then I'm moving in."

Tillie crept around the back of the barn, keeping to the shadows. Just as she was about to edge around a corner, she noticed a small piece of wood, nailed to the structure. It looked like it had been put there to patch a hole. She tapped on her com. "I think I found a way in." She tugged at the board. It didn't move. "But I need a pry bar." She looked around but found nothing useful.

Something landed next to her. It was a small Swiss army knife. Tillie inspected the tools it contained and pulled out the nail file. Not ideal, but maybe she could make it work. She pried at the nails used to affix the board and slowly removed a few. Then she slid the knife in between the barn and the board and pulled. The board popped free and she set it on the ground. She stuck her head through the hole. "Dammit," she muttered. "Empty."

The house had also been empty. Maybe no one was on the farm at all. She had not heard any sounds. No humans. No animals. Strange.

"Only two more to go," Abdul responded.

Tillie grunted. There was no way the other barns would have similar openings. Staying close to the ground, she crawled to the next barn. Before she even slid through the door, she sensed it was empty. There were no lights or noises that indicated the presence of living beings. The next barn was on the other side of the yard. Running across the open area was too risky. She would have to stick to the wooded perimeter. Groaning softly, Tillie crawled into the brush. Carefully, she stood and brushed off the sticks and leaves that had become embedded in her ninja suit. Then she bent over at the waist and ran to the back of the third barn.

It quickly became evident that the structure was not empty. Tillie heard what sounded like a woman crying. Then another began to wail. "Hush up," a deep voice said. "Crying ain't going to get you out of here. How do you think I feel? I'm used to sleeping in a bed. I ain't never been put in a barn, chained to a stall, left to sleep in the hay. This is degrading. Unless you can help us get out of here, shut your pie hole."

"Oh, leave them be," said someone said with a posh British accent. "They are new here. Soon enough, they will learn what it is like to be an animal. There is no backing out once you commit."

Another wail went up.

Tillie searched the backside of the barn for an opening. She found nothing. She gazed at the second story of the barn. There was a large door up there. It probably provided access to a hayloft. The door was shut but slightly ajar. Maybe she could rappel up the wall and enter through there. She tapped her com. "I found them. Well, some anyway. Third barn, the one across the yard. I'm going to need some help rappelling into the hayloft." She dropped to the ground and picked at the foundation. The barn was set on a cement slab. "Possibly a couple of agents with axes."

"Axes, not shovels?"

"If we can't get in through the hayloft, we might have to create an opening in the back wall. Looks like the barn is built on a cement slab, so there is no way to tunnel in. To avoid the cameras in front of the barn, we need to get these people out the back way."

"What if there are cameras in the barn?"

Tillie ignored Abdul's question. She would be surprised if there were any cameras in the barn. "It sounds like they are tied to their stalls, maybe even chained. We are going to need some clippers, bolt cutters, and possibly, lock pics."

Abdul persisted. "Are you sure there is no guard in there? Secure the barn, first, then we move in. I will not put my team at risk."

Damn that man. Did he think she was an agent-in-training? Tillie bit her lip, an attempt to measure her words. Finally, she said, "Get me a hook and rope, and I will secure the building. And someone needs to be posted as guard. I do not want

Abernathy's friends creeping up on us."

After a moment, Abdul appeared from the shadows. He handed her a rope and hook, then a small extending rope ladder. "Once we get them free, we may want to start moving them out by ladder, rather than waiting for someone to break down the wall."

"We?"

Abdul cocked an eyebrow. "Did you think I was going to allow you to go in alone?" He tapped what looked like large scissors attached to his belt. "Let's get moving."

Tillie pitched the hook at the hayloft but it didn't catch and fell to the ground. She tried again. This time it caught. Tillie pulled on it to ensure it was secure, then wrapped the end of the rope around her waist. Hand over hand, she crawled up the building to the door. She opened it slowly, worried about the door creaking. It opened smoothly and she pulled herself into the loft.

Swiftly, she untied the rope around her waist, checked that it was still wedged safely into the door frame, and threw it down to Abdul. Then she crawled across the floor to the edge of the loft and looked down. She recognized some as having participated in the live auction, but there were a few newcomers. Some of them were isolated in separate stalls, but the twins she had attempted to purchase at auction were together. All were chained to railings. From her position in the loft, she could see no guards. She also could not see Lady Annabelle.

Directly beneath her was a Hucow, a Holstein, with all the markings tattooed on her skin. She was sat quietly, saying nothing. Tillie dropped a piece of hay on her head and she looked up. Tillie quickly held a finger over her lips, indicating that the Hucow should remain silent. Carefully, Tillie mouthed, "Any guards?" The Hucow shook her head.

Tillie grasped the edge of the loft and flipped herself over, dropping to the floor. Everyone fell silent and stared at her.

Again, Tillie held a finger to her lips. The bull used his head to point at a single camera in the barn, which was located over a sliding barn door. She slid along the wall until she was behind it. From its position, she deduced it was placed to record people entering the barn, not to monitor the prisoners. However, there was no way to tell if the camera had sound capabilities. She walked back to the prisoners and whispered, "Keep the noise down. They may be monitoring for sound."

A ladder dropped down from the loft and Abdul crawled down. He began to move around the room, cutting through the chains. Tillie followed him and explained to each person that they needed to climb up to the loft, where they would be assisted to the ground outside. Two more agents came down the ladder and someone threw a gurney to the ground. Good. Her agents had been perceptive enough to realize that not all would be capable of climbing a rope ladder.

One by one, they asked the people if they were in the barn willingly. Those that wished to stay behind were left in their pens, chains removed. The other hu-animals crawled up the rope ladder to the loft or were tied to the gurney and carried up.

When Tillie got to a well-built bull, she asked, "Have you seen the Hucow from the auction? The one wearing the crown? I believe she was transported here with you."

The bull frowned. In an American accent, he responded, "You mean the hoity-toity chick? Haven't seen her. She was in the truck but didn't get off with the rest of us. I heard one of the guys say something about a *special delivery*." He waggled his eyebrows. "Just assumed she went with one of the drivers for a little playtime."

Tillie's heart sank. "The house is empty. Any idea where they could have taken her?"

The bull shook his head. "Hey, we're not even sure how we wound up here. It's not like they're going to give us any of the details. I have no idea where we're headed. Frankly, she's not my concern." He shrugged.

"You are American?"

The bull nodded. "Georgia born and bred."

Tillie stared at him. "So, you were kidnapped in America and shipped here?"

The bull shook his head. "Not really. I volunteered. I'm looking for my sister. She was snatched over six months ago. Everyone I talked to told me these guys had her, but I couldn't get anyone *official* interested, so I worked my way in. Entered their *training* program. Went from a teacher to a sex worker overnight." He grunted. "I suppose some men would enjoy this work. I don't." Sadness entered his eyes. "When I heard about the auction, I figured it was my last chance. No one has seen her." He waved a hand over his enlarged cock and balls. "And this sucks big time." He sighed. "Anyway, I'm ready to head home. Call it a day."

Tillie studied him. "I can't believe you couldn't get the authorities involved."

He snorted. "No offense, but I couldn't get the *authorities* to care. They don't have the time, much less the inclination to look for a poor little Black girl from rural Georgia. If I was white, they would have—"

Tillie steered him toward an agent. "Agent Throkes, when you take this man's information, get the details on his sister's disappearance." She smiled at him. "I've got friends in America who will help."

The bull hugged her. A tear dropped down his cheek. "First time in a long time I've felt any hope." He gazed at Agent Throkes. "I hope you can find some pants I can fit into."

Chapter Six: Where in the World is Lady Annabelle?

Tillie pulled out her phone and punched a button. Lord Ryder answered immediately.

"Agent Spencer, you are keeping late hours these days."

"I'm sorry to disturb you, sir, but I need your assistance. We found some of the people from the auction, but Lady Annabelle wasn't with them."

Lord Ryder harrumphed. "And what do you make of that?"

"Well, we discounted it, but there is still a possibility that Lady Annabelle was sold to *Marwolaeth I'r Frenhines*, sir."

Lord Ryder cleared his throat. "Death to the Monarchy? Oh my, this will not do, not at all. I shall have to inform the Queen."

Tillie swiped at a fly. "And in the meantime, I need someone on the ports and private charters to and from *Eire*. If The Mars get their hands on Lady Annabelle, we may never get her back, at least alive."

"How convenient that Agent Ali is your partner."

"Sir?"

"Because we need help from his brother. He has already faced down these terrorists. He will know where they can be found, and more importantly, he can follow the money to verify that The Mars have Lady Annabelle. Yes, Sheikh Harun Ali must be contacted immediately."

Tillie walked into an MISix conference center and gazed at the occupants.

Sheikh Harun Ali and his American wife, Marianne Benson, were seated at the table. Two of the utmost experts on international terrorism, they were said to have created a database superior to that of the world's intelligence agencies, including Interpol and MISix. They were both attorneys who regularly sought recompense from terrorists, terrorist organizations, and their supporters on behalf of the victims of terrorist acts. Not only did they have information on every terrorist organization in the world, but they also had access to their financial networks.

They were fearless and feared, and they were on the speed dial of every leader in the free world. Somehow, they had managed to remain below the radar by living on a farm in Wisconsin, until Marwolaeth I'r Frenhines had invaded their life, burying a plane in an adjacent cornfield, passengers still aboard. After attempts to murder the couple and their daughter failed, the group decided to blow up the plane. Untended, the resulting fire could have destroyed their farm and possibly taken their lives as well.

Tillie knew they would be an invaluable resource in her search for Lady Annabelle. The only problem was, they hated her. *Personally.* Several years ago, both the British and the Americans attempted to rescue an author being held captive, one of *the disappeared* — people held under house arrest for allegedly posing a threat to a government or political group. The woman was a member of one of the ruling families in the UAE. She had written a book that detailed the UAE's involvement in terrorism, citing personal and overheard conversations. When the Americans managed to successfully rescue the woman, Tillie had attempted to create a diversion that would permit her to snatch the woman and bring her back to England. That diversion involved contacting Sheikh Ali's son—who had placed a bounty on his father and sister after they disavowed Shariah law and became American citizens—and informed him of Agent Hope Ali's whereabouts in the UAE.

Hope's role in the rescue was to masquerade as the writer and lead her captives on a merry chase. Unfortunately, she ran directly into an angry mob organized by her brother. Hope was left bloody and broken, and she barely survived.

Abdul swept into the room behind her. He nodded at his brother. "Harun, good to see you again. How ironic that it is over the same organization that brought us together the last time." He pulled Tillie toward the table. "This is my partner, Agent Tillie Spencer."

Harun stood and hugged his brother. Then he turned to Tillie. His gaze was steady, but his eyes were cold. "Forgive me if I cannot give you a similarly warm welcome, but my wife and I have not yet recovered from the brutal attack on our daughter."

"Harun." Marianne Benson spoke softly, but her gaze was fierce. "I believe Hope and the Agency have settled the matter. You don't need to pursue it further." She turned to Abdul and smiled. "I am pleased to see you, Abdul." She cocked an eyebrow. "Though for a while there, the rumor was that you had gone rogue and were dancing with the devil."

Abdul laughed. "I may dance with the devil occasionally, but that does not mean he owns my soul. I am still slaving away for the Queen." He smiled at Mari. "Thank you for coming so quickly."

"Well, it's hard to ignore a summons from the Queen, and when your husband has a plane, it is much easier to respond quickly." Mari motioned to the chairs at the table. "Please sit. Let's get down to business. It was made clear that time was of the essence."

Everyone sat, and Mari walked over to a control panel set

into a console. She pushed a button, and a whiteboard lit up. "As you know, after we rescued the people off Flight Eight Seven Zero and The Mars were prosecuted, Dianna and Anders interviewed them extensively at Guantanamo Bay. We were able to collect a considerable amount of information on the organization, its members, and its financing."

Twelve photos appeared on the screen. "These are the current members of Marwolaeth I'r Frenhines. Six are incarcerated at Guantanamo, three have been released, and three are recruits."

Tillie leaned forward and studied the faces. It always amazed her how normal terrorists appeared. There was nothing in their faces to indicate that they were evil. Most were smiling in their photos. However, the tell was in the eyes. They were stone cold.

Mari pointed at the photos of those recently released. "These three have been fairly quiet. We could not detect any significant communication or contact between them and the new members, which makes me think this may be a new group that merely adopted the name." She brought up a few more photos. "These gentlemen are believed to be the financiers of the new order."

Tillie studied the group and gasped. "But that's a former member of Parliament."

Harun nodded. "And someone who wishes to dissolve the Monarchy. Apparently, he has put his money where his mouth is." Another screen popped up. A bank statement.

Abdul cleared his throat. "Fifty million pounds? That's pretty significant. Has this been verified?"

Harun gazed at Abdul. "I'm afraid so. We have transfers to the account, bank acknowledgments, and proof the newest members of The Mars have been drawing on these funds."

Mari pulled up another screen. "Though we were a little puzzled by their purchases until now. We thought they had gone into farming." She pointed at an invoice. "Everything you need to raise a cow, or in this case, a human cow."

Tillie hugged herself and shuddered. "Lady Annabelle is most certainly in their sights."

Mari gazed at her husband and nodded. Harun opened a file he had set in front of him. "Apparently, it is much worse. There were also several purchases for the care of an infant. Either Lady Annabelle is pregnant, or they intend to impregnate her."

Abdul slammed his fist on the table. "Bloody hell. A royal baby? The Queen would move heaven and earth to protect her own blood. What a crafty way to manipulate her for their own purposes. She would be damned no matter how she responded. That could end the monarchy."

Tillie stood. "I think I'm going to be sick." She stepped back from the table and started to move toward the door. Then she swayed and propped herself up against the wall.

Abdul grabbed her and forced her to sit in her chair. "Head between your knees, darling. Take deep breaths." He patted her head. "Deep breaths, Tillie."

Tillie felt her stomach begin to settle and raised her head. Tears began to flow. "They want to kill the Monarchy and destroy the Queen. I can't let that happen. I have worked too hard to protect it. We must find Lady Annabelle and bring her home safely."

Abdul pulled her into his arms. Gently, he soothed her, rubbing her back, kissing the top of her head. Mari and Harun stared at him, but he shook his head. "Despite everything, I love this woman and I will not permit anyone to harm her. Make no mistake, harming the Queen in any way would destroy Tillie, especially if on her watch. If she fails at this mission, she will not survive." His face turned stormy. "That will not happen as long I am at her side. I am going to take these pathetic slags down."

Abdul studied Tillie. She was curled up on their bed, the covers pulled up to her neck. "Feeling better?"

Tillie groaned and pulled a pillow over her head. "Oh, God, I am so embarrassed. I had a complete meltdown in front of your brother and his wife. They must think I am barmy."

Abdul sat down on the bed and pulled the pillow off her face. He kissed her. "For God's sake, darling, you're human — though you pretend not to be. This situation is horrifying." He tugged at a strand of her blonde hair. "Sometimes, a good cry can do one a world of good. It is a great stress reliever."

"But in front of your brother?"

"Believe it or not, if you had to break down in front of someone, I am glad it was him and Mari. Those two have been through the wringer. They understand the pressure you are under. They also know what is at stake. If you had broken down in front of your team, the results would have been devastating, on morale and your command. You can bet Ryder would have called you in for a mandatory psychological evaluation."

Tillie groaned again, then sat up. "Still, it was embarrassing. I pride myself on keeping a tight rein on my emotions. It is essential in my job."

Abdul rubbed her shoulders and she stretched her spine. "True, but sometimes you need to get it out. And other times, you need to share it with me. Stop keeping it all bottled up. We are partners. We are supposed to share — everything."

Tillie sighed. "I know, but these feelings are new. My parents did not do emotions. With eight kids, they had no time. If one of us let loose, they told us to suck it up and move on."

Abdul chuckled. "Why am I not surprised? The first time I met your father, I knew he was a tough nut, and your mother, well, she still won't look me in the eyes. It is pretty obvious they had someone different in mind for you. Someone whiter, less foreign."

Tillie turned and nestled into his chest. She emitted a deep sigh. "They *are* pretty set in their ways. In their world, people stick with their own kind. I imagine bringing someone of a different color into their home shocked them to their core. It's not that they are prejudiced. It's just that they are rarely exposed to people who are not white." She smiled slightly. "Though I suspect if you had worn a thaub and keffiyeh, my mum would be all over you. She has a real Lawrence of Arabia fantasy."

Abdul grinned. "Peter O'Toole wore dark makeup to make him appear dark-skinned, hardly a true Arab."

Tillie ran a finger through the thick black hair on his chest. "I'm just saying, if she saw you as a Sheikh, rather than a colleague who works with me at a mythical corporation, she would view you more favorably. A Sheikh she can relate to. A Brown man in a suit? Not at all."

"Wow, so if I dress up the way she thinks an Arab should, she will accept me? Must I also lead a camel around on a leash?" He shook his head. "That is all kinds of wrong."

Tillie smirked. "Call it racism without intent. No one has ever disputed her thinking, so she has no idea she is being offensive. All she knows is that you are different. That's enough to make her suspicious." She pulled on his chest hair. "Besides, it doesn't matter what she thinks. All that matters is what I think."

Abdul kissed her and gazed into her eyes. "And what do you think, my love?"

"That you are the biggest pain in the arse I have ever met, but for some reason, I am madly in love with you."

"And if I ask you to be my wife? What would you think of that?"

"That it's too soon. We are too new. We need more time."

Abdul chortled. "I do not understand how a woman who

busts balls for a living can be such a chicken in her personal life. We've worked together for more than five years and have been an exclusive couple for two, living together for one. You are like a scared little bunny rabbit running away from the big bad wolf." He grinned. "Face it, you have commitment issues. You are afraid you are going to turn into your mother, stuck at home with eight kids. That's understandable, but let me tell you a secret." He stage-whispered, "If we have children, we will stop at two, even if I must visit a surgeon to be . . ." He manipulated two fingers into scissors and snipped.

Tillie giggled. "Every time my mum wound up preggers, she threatened to do the same to my dad, without the surgeon. But no, I do not have commitment issues. I just know I will have to make adjustments if we marry and have children, and I am not ready for that yet. Give me a few more years to sow my wild oats, as they say."

Abdul raised his eyebrows. "Sow your wild oats, as in other men? That is not happening."

Tillie laughed. "I worded that poorly. I meant gain other life experiences. For example, I would like to sleep under the stars somewhere in Africa, maybe in an elephant habitat. Or spend a few weeks in Tahiti running around starkers, being wild and free of all of life's problems."

"Alone?"

She snuggled into him again. "No, with you. But without worrying about a baby at home. I want to spend time free of all responsibilities, doing what I want, when I want." She gazed at him. "When this is over, I want to take a long sabbatical and think about what I want to do with the rest of my life. And how you fit into that life."

"Dammit, Tillie. That sounds like a brush-off."

She shook her head. "Not at all. Think about it. Most of our time together is on assignment. We have never really spent time being anything other than colleagues. I think we need more personal time together, without the constraints of the job. I don't even know if we could survive a two-week vacation alone."

"Yet we live together. Surely that means something."

"We are compatible, as *work* colleagues and roommates. We are used to each other, so we are comfortable living together. What if we no longer worked together? Could we survive?"

Abdul ran a hand through his thick hair. "I would like to think so. Tillie, I know you inside and out. Probably better than most couples do, because I have seen you at your best and your worst. I love you, but more importantly, I understand you. I think that puts us light years ahead of people whose relationship developed in more traditional ways." He stroked her arm. "You have never questioned our relationship before. Why start now? Where is all of this doubt coming from?"

Tillie moaned. "Because for the first time, my future is in doubt. What if I can't find Lady Annabelle? What if the terrorists win and that causes the fall of the Monarchy? My failure could have a devastating impact on my Queen, my country, even our relationship. Would you even want to associate with an agent who single-handedly destroyed our world? You would be tarred with the same brush because we work together. This could not only destroy me but also you. Have you considered that?"

Abdul kissed the top of her head. "May I remind you that we are in this together? No matter what happens, you are not in this alone. You have a whole team behind you. If you fail, we all fail, and as far as I am concerned, failure is not even a possibility. I will accept failure upon my death."

Tillie swiped at a tear. "The Queen asked for me, personally. I answer only to her."

Abdul chuckled. "And you think if we fail, she will call for your beheading? Look, we are human. We can only do what is humanly possible. Yes, we will do everything we can to rescue Lady Annabelle. But if we fail, it is because her rescue was not humanly possible."

Tillie tried to smile. "I know that, but this time, we are up against terrorists who make Prince Mustapha look like a wimp. The Mars are pure evil. They will stop at nothing to achieve their goals. Even bury a plane full of passengers in a cornfield."

Abdul kissed her gently. "The Americans stopped them. We can, too. Stop thinking we are the David to their Goliath. It is the other way around. The Mars are not infallible, and we shall prove that."

CHAPTER SEVEN: DIVERSIONS

Tillie watched the blip move across the map on the white-board.

She turned to her team. "The truck we believe is transport-ing Lady Annabelle appears to be headed to Blackpool, where there are ferries to Dublin or Belfast. It is currently approxi-mately twenty-five kilometers away from that port. I have sent Agent Struthers and Wilkes ahead to determine the in-tended destination and to verify that Lady Annabelle is aboard. Once we receive that confirmation, we will move in."

A young agent raised her hand. "What if she is not on the lorry?"

Tillie studied the woman. Elise Madison. Young, beautiful, perky, and the top of her class at Fort Monckton in Ports-mouth, one of the agency's primary training centers. She was known to be ambitious and a little too enthusiastic. Tillie was warned that she needed to keep a tight rein on the woman. She had a streak of impulsiveness that had not yet been tem-pered by age. "We are tracking all of the truck traffic to and from Abernathy's farms near York and Manchester. As you know, Lady Annabelle was not at Manchester, so we had an-other team closely monitoring the farm at York. She was seen there."

In a tone that bordered on obstinate, Elise replied, "She was seen there, once? How do we know she is still there? How do we know she is on that lorry? Was she seen?"

Tillie hesitated and silently counted to ten. It would not be wise to allow the new agent to goad her. "Whoever entered that truck was covered with a blanket. So, no, we are not absolutely positive she is on board. However, we are also monitoring transmissions from the farm, and those communications have led us to believe that she is being moved. *Today.* That is the only truck to leave Abernathy Farms in the past forty-eight hours. We missed her during the raid, but she has been seen since, so we have been monitoring all exit checkpoints, as well as all of Abernathy Farms' freight ships and planes. We are confident that Lady Annabelle has not passed through regular migration channels. We have to work with the information we have."

Elise frowned. She took a deep breath as if centering herself. "But Abernathy took a runner stateside . . ."

Tillie planted her feet and gazed at the agent, her mouth set in a firm line. She could not believe the cheek of this woman. "American immigration control boarded his plane in Boston and conducted an intensive search. Only he and his executive assistant were aboard. And believe me, the Americans took that plane apart."

Elise leaned forward, her voice growing strident. "Our job is to prove facts. I see no facts in evidence here. What about when Abernathy landed in Dallas? Did someone search his plane again? He could have been hiding Lady Annabelle, even disguised her as his assistant."

Tillie allowed herself a slight smile. "I assure you the Yanks are on it. They had agents on the ground in both Boston and Dallas. They even followed Abernathy to his residence and have posted watch at his farm and business offices. It is being handled."

Elise's eyes narrowed. "My concern is that we are being led on a wild goose chase. We have people racing around the country, searching for a woman no one has seen in five days. That seems odd, doesn't it? Someone should have seen her by now."

Abdul snorted. "Why do I think you drove your parents crazy insisting there was no Santa Claus? Did you force them to escort you to Lapland to prove that he did not exist?"

The other agents in the room chuckled, and Elise's face reddened. "I am just concerned that we are wasting agency resources . . ."

Abdul waved her off. "Ah, to be young again and oh, so innocent." He glared at her. "When Agent Spencer is on the job, you can be sure she has covered all the angles and ferreted out any and all available information. Questioning a superior — no, questioning an agent far superior to you, borders on insolence, Agent Madison. I advise you to watch your tongue."

Elise threw up her hands in a gesture of surrender. "I apologize, I did not mean to imply — "

"Yet, you did imply it." Abdul snapped. He turned to Tillie. "Agent Spencer, please continue."

She nodded at Abdul, then hit a button on the console and an aerial photo appeared on the whiteboard. "As I was about to say, the Yanks have set up comprehensive surveillance on Mr. Abernathy. Several phone intercepts have led them to conclude that Lady Annabelle was still in the U.K."

Abdul steepled his fingers. "Either willingly or unwillingly. Lady Anabelle appeared to be so deformed at the auction that she may not wish to be rescued. She may resist. She may resent that she was not found sooner. Or, she may be incapable of cooperating in a covert rescue. Those are all contingencies you must plan for."

"Which is why when we do find her, be prepared to sedate and extract," Tillie added. "That may be the most expeditious approach."

The helicopter hovered about a kilometer behind the ferry, moving in and out of clouds in the sky to obscure its presence.

Tillie kept her binoculars trained on the ship, while the four other agents checked their parachutes and other equipment. She turned to Abdul and frowned.

"I am pretty sure they are off-course." Tillie lowered her binoculars. "They seem to be drifting toward the Isle of Man rather than Ireland. That's not on the schedule. The ferry is supposed to head directly to Belfast. So, either they are experiencing an emergency, or they're being paid to divert course."

"Or being forced to divert. Anyone could be on that ferry, including The Mars." Abdul adjusted the helicopter's path. He peered out the windshield. "Really, Man is a perfect place to hide or to be hidden, especially for terrorists. It's isolated, not heavily trafficked. People keep to themselves. That may be where The Mars has been hiding all along."

Tillie played with her binoculars. "We need to board that ferry before it docks at Mann—otherwise, we may meet even more resistance."

Abdul nodded. "That would be my guess. There is not much wind at the moment. I can drop you on board, right next to the pilothouse. There do not appear to be any shooters around, but I suggest you land, locked and loaded. They may all be hiding in the pilothouse."

Tillie sighed. "Can we radio the ferry, at least get a sense of what sort of welcome is waiting?"

"I can try." Abdul flipped a switch and spoke into his headset. "Control? We are tracking a ferry departing Blackpool, heading to Belfast. They seem to be drifting off course, maybe even preparing to make an unscheduled stop. Can you ask the Coastguard to do a check-in?"

The radio crackled and someone said, "Will do." The radio went silent for a few moments. "Negative ACORN Ten A. The ferry is not responding to radio alerts. Their communications system appears to be inoperative. Please advise."

Abdul groaned. "Control, suggest Coastguard intervention before we intercept the ship. Unfriendlies may be aboard. Advise caution."

The controller grunted. "Let's hope they aren't monitoring this frequency. Wait for confirmation please."

Tillie gazed at Abdul. "Please tell me we don't have to wait for the Coastguard before boarding."

"Probably not, but they will make a great diversion so you can land safely. I would rather have the guns trained on them, not you."

The controller broke into their conversation. "ACORN Ten A, the Coastguard is nearby. They will board the ship but are requesting air backup. They want you in place to surveil before they board. The last ferry they boarded was carrying a bomb. They are a bit twitchy."

Abdul rubbed his eyes and frowned. "Thank you, Control. We will provide air and ground support as requested." He shook his head. "I hate being out in the open like a sitting duck. The Coastguard wants us there so they will shoot at us not them. It might be safer to board now. Take them by surprise."

Tillie nodded. "Drop us right next to the pilot room."

He angled his head toward their team. "Think they can handle it?"

"They've been trained by the best. Of course, they can handle it. Besides, these new suits are bulletproof. The only thing not protected is the eyes and those are covered by goggles. It would take a superior marksman to take one of my team down."

"What about the terrorists? You don't think they'll be similarly attired?"

They reached the ferry and Abdul made a circular sweep. No guns were visible, but he knew that meant nothing. He moved the helicopter until it was positioned about three feet from the deck.

Tillie turned to her team, all of whom were already preparing for the drop. "This is a short drop. Hit the ground running. After we have subdued any unfriendlies, we will get to work. Sanders and Madison, you search for Lady Annabelle. Start with the truck. Hansen and Brookstone, you're with me." She rolled back the helicopter door and moved into position. She gazed at Abdul and nodded. *"Ahbak."* Which meant I *love you* in Arabic. Then Tillie jumped out of the helicopter onto the deck, keeping low to avoid the rotors. The rest of her team followed.

Tillie removed the goggles from her head and peeled back the body armor to reveal her sweat-matted hair. She shook her locks, then peered off into the distance, toward the Isle of Man. "Dammit, where did they go?"

"Maybe they slipped into the sea unnoticed?" Elise Madison also removed body armor from her head. "We saw them board, so either they are hiding very well, or they slipped into the sea. Maybe there were wetsuits on the lorry and the whole purpose of moving close to Mann was to allow them to swim to shore."

Tillie spoke into her communications device. "Agent Ali, please make a sweep of the dock on the Isle of Man. See if any deep-sea divers crawled up onto the beach."

"On it." Abdul waved as he pulled away from the ferry.

The Coastguard ship drifted up to the ferry. Tillie strode toward them and stopped in front of the first man off the ship. He appeared to be the officer in charge. She flashed her credentials. "Everyone appears to be unarmed, but we need a comprehensive sweep to make sure there is nothing hidden on board. Also, the people we are pursuing are not present. Either they are hiding or they somehow escaped."

The officer pointed at the truck. "Did you search the lorry

for any hidden compartments? Anything that could hide a bomb, or even a body?"

Tillie gestured toward the truck. "Madison and Saunders, take apart that vehicle. Strip it down to its frame, if need be. You are looking for anything and everything that suggests our target was on board."

Madison and Saunders hurried to the lorry and disappeared inside.

She turned back to the officer. She had purposely avoided mentioning Lady Annabelle by name. The Coastguard was not entitled to the details of her mission. "The rest of my team will help search, but I am the officer in charge. They act on my command."

"Understood." He barked out an order, and twelve people in uniform, all wearing tactical vests and carrying weapons, streamed on board. The officer issued instructions and his team began to search the cars on deck. Tillie waved at the rest of her team and they went below.

Someone yelled, "Got something, sir."

Tillie and the Coastguard officer made their way to a large empty container. A Coastguard member held up what looked like a glove. "Not sure what this is, but it was caught in the corner."

Tillie took it from him and examined it. It was a glove without fingers but split into two halves to resemble a cloven hoof. Just like the one Lady Annabelle had been wearing at auction. She pulled an evidence bag from her tool belt and dropped the glove inside. "Our target was here. She might still be on board. We need to check everything — All of the vehicles, containers, toilets, lifeboats, closets, engine rooms, and anything else that could be used to hide a person." She walked to the railing and peered into the water. "And I need someone to go into the water to check the hull. See if there is anything attached or floating nearby."

The chief officer nodded at two coastguards and issued the order. The men scrambled back onto the Coastguard ship and a few minutes later emerged wearing scuba gear. The officer nodded at them and they slipped into the water. He turned to the rest of his crew. "Let's tear this ship apart. Look for anything that can hold a person, and search for any hidden compartments below." The officer turned to Tillie. "If your victim is here, we will find her."

Tillie gazed at him. "Thank you. Your assistance is much appreciated." Her com beeped and she covered her ears to shut out the noise.

"Tillie, four people in scuba gear, carrying a body bag, just emerged on a beach near Douglas." Abdul's voice sounded strained.

"Were they apprehended?"

"Negative. I didn't have enough time to get the authorities on board. I'm still trying to get clearance to land. They are not fond of outsiders."

"Well, just follow them then. See where they hole up."

Abdul paused. "Negative. I need to refuel. I am in the red zone already. If I stay in the air much longer, I am going to take a dive into the sea."

"Do it, then get back in the air. Maybe —"

A loud siren started wailing in the background and her com cut out. Tillie frowned. The com crackled and she heard Abdul say, "Going . . . try . . . land." Then silence. Tillie's heart dropped into her shoes. Abdul was a skilled pilot, but he was not able to magically refuel. And if his copter ran out of gas before he could land safely . . . She sighed. *No, he would land safely. He would be safe.* She could not imagine any other outcome. Tillie shook herself out of that negative thought. She needed to focus on *her* objective.

Tillie watched Elise crawl under the unmarked brown lorry. "Need a little help here, God," she muttered. "We are being blocked at every turn and someone's life is in peril. Your intervention is needed." She walked toward the lorry and shouted, "Anything?"

Saunders gazed at her. "Found a false floor, enough room for several people. We are checking to see whether someone can move out through the bottom and escape."

Elise slid out from under the truck. "No visible latch on the outside, but there is a hinged seam, so it must open some way. Maybe it is electronically controlled?"

"Possibly. But right now, we are looking for a body." Tillie's thoughts turned to Abdul's report of a body bag. If Lady Annabelle *had been* on board, she could have been spirited away in a body bag, which could mean all the alterations to her body rendered her unable to swim, or she was dead. Tillie could only hope it was the former.

CHAPTER EIGHT: THE BARN

Tillie pushed on the barn door and it opened without a sound. "Strange that the door was not locked." She reached for her handgun. "That always makes me nervous."

Abdul guided her into the barn. "Or maybe Lady Annabelle never made it this far, so they do not need to lock up."

They had managed to track the people who swam to the Isle of Man to this farm. Her team had entered the compound at nightfall, skillfully disarming the people in residence. After the team questioned those detained and learned nothing, they searched the farmhouse. There was no evidence of Lady Annabelle anywhere. Now a search of the grounds was underway.

As a team, they moved through the barn, systematically checking each stall. All were filled with livestock. All bovine. None human. When they reached the last stall, Tillie sighed. "It's like she disappeared into thin air. Was this simply a distraction?"

Abdul gestured toward the corner of the barn and tapped his ear. Tillie listened. Over the moos of the cows, she heard a woman crying. They moved to the wall and began to push against it. It was solid. There were no doors. No give at all.

Tillie stopped and listened again. She took a few steps away from the wall. Then she dropped to her knees and pressed her ear to the dirt floor. Hurriedly, she cleared away the soil, looking for a trapdoor. "Hello? Is someone there?" She waited for an answer. The keening stopped, but there was no other response. She turned to Abdul. "There has to be a door somewhere." She continued to clear away the dirt. The fact that Lady Annabelle might have been buried alive terrified her.

Abdul joined her. Together they swept away dirt but found only more dirt. Tillie sat up. *Where could Lady Annabelle be?* She stood and brushed off her jeans. "Do you think there's an entrance in one of the other stalls?"

"Or perhaps a root cellar? A place they store vegetables in winter? Before we waste our time digging around these stalls, perhaps we should survey the outside of the building." Abdul started to walk out of the barn. "Give me a few minutes to check."

Tillie hurried after him. "I want to be there when Lady Annabelle is found."

They walked around the building until they came upon a set of doors set into the ground. Tillie again drew her handgun. "I'll cover you." She positioned herself behind him, slightly off to the side to ensure she would have a clear shot. By law, MISix was not permitted to carry guns within the UK, but on the Isle of Man, firearms were legal. Therefore, they were permitted as a defensive measure. Tillie was not a fan of guns—most of her work involved information gathering and analysis, but she did believe in the need for sufficient weaponry when facing a gun-toting enemy. Anything less was futile.

Abdul nodded. He removed his gun and reached for the handle on one of the doors. He flung it open and a woman screamed. "Quiet," he hissed. "We are here to help you." He opened the other door, and leading with his gun, he carefully stepped down a set of wooden steps. Then he disappeared.

Tillie moved to the top of the stairs. Damn. There was no light in the cellar. She could see nothing. How was she supposed to protect Abdul?

A few moments later, his head popped back up. Abdul

placed his gun back in his holster and gazed at Tillie. "There is a woman tied up down there, but I can't see shite. And she's not talking."

Tillie put her weapon away and pulled a small flashlight off of her belt "Maybe she has no desire to talk to a man. Let me try." She turned on the light and stepped into the cellar. It was cold and dark. Tillie swept the room with her flashlight, finding nothing but shelves mounted against dirt walls, all containing jars and baskets of some sort of vegetables. In the middle of the cellar, a woman sat, her hands tied to a large wooden beam. The woman's head was bowed, intentionally hidden in shadow. Her body was covered in some sort of loose-fitting jumpsuit.

Tillie drew closer. She knelt before the woman and reached out to get a better look at her face. Without warning, the woman lunged at her and knocked the light out of her hands. It bounced off the floor and blinked out. "Dammit, we are trying to help you here. I am with the Secret Intelligence Service, MISix." Tillie stepped back and squinted at the woman, trying to see her in the faint light streaming through the open doors. "Look, you can identify yourself or I can knock you out and drag you out of here, and fingerprint you. You can make this easy or make this hard."

Abdul knelt next to her. "What Agent Spencer meant to say is, we are simply here to rescue any British citizens being held against their will. If you don't fit within that definition, we will leave."

Slowly, the woman lifted her head and stared at them. Tillie could barely make out the blonde hair and bovine ears. "Lady Annabelle Travers, I presume?"

The woman nodded. In a very posh accent, with a decided lisp—no doubt created by her enlarged lips—she demanded, "Take me to the Queen."

"First, we need to get you out of here." Abdul pulled out a

knife and began to cut through her bindings. When Lady Annabelle was free, he lifted her out of the cellar. Abdul set her on the ground and motioned to the burlap bag that encased her body. "We need to get you out of there so you can walk, unless you would prefer to remain covered."

Lady Annabelle's head swiveled somewhat manically, taking in her surroundings. "I am afraid I am at a disadvantage here. I would prefer to keep this on. Perhaps you can cut an opening for my feet?"

Abdul knelt beside her and cut the bottom of the bag, holding it open so Lady Annabelle could stand. After he helped her to her cloven feet, somewhat awkwardly, he turned to Tillie. "Let's get her out of here."

"My plan, exactly." Tillie barked into her com. "Air support? Commence retrieval. Subject has been rescued. She is alive."

Lady Annabelle's face contorted. She appeared to be trying to frown, but her overly large lips, no doubt Botox-enhanced, seemed to make it difficult. "The only one who must know what has happened is Aunt Lilabet." The Queen's closest relatives often referred to her as Lilabet, rather than Elizabeth.

Tillie gazed at Lady Annabelle. "Can you walk? We need to get to a pickup point. I don't want to stay here. There may be a few surprise guests coming, and it is best we move out."

Lady Annabelle plopped back onto the ground and peeled the very realistic hooves off of her feet. Underneath were normal toes. They were red and bruised but did not appear to have been surgically altered. She handed the prosthetics to Abdul. "No evidence left behind, I'm sure." She stood and winced. "Let's go."

A shot rang out in the distance. Then another. Lady Annabelle looked toward the sound, her eyes wide with panic.

Abdul gestured toward a wooded area. "As old Holmes was prone to say, *the game is afoot.* Let's get out of here."

All three ran for the trees, zigging and zagging to avoid bullets.

"Use your guns, people." Lady Annabelle stopped and glared at Tillie. "They are going to shoot us."

"No time." Tillie pushed the woman through the forest. "That would slow us down. We have to get to the clearing ahead for pickup."

Lady Annabelle shrieked as a bullet hit a nearby tree, then she ran.

The helicopter was waiting in a small meadow in the midst of the forest. Tillie pulled Lady Annabelle into the aircraft. Just as they scrambled into their seats, a bullet struck the helicopter. Abdul looked out the window. "There's four of them bearing down on us. All armed." He turned to the pilot. "Get us the hell out of here, Harvey. I don't relish being the target on a shooting range. The last time some terrorists got this close, I barely escaped with my dick."

Without a word, Harvey handed Abdul an automatic rifle. Abdul slammed the hatch closed and opened a window. As the copter lifted into the air, he returned fire. A few more bullets pinged off the aircraft, pitching the copter to the left and right, but Harvey managed to keep control and flew away. When they passed over a copse of trees, the ground fire stopped.

Harvey expelled a deep breath. "Dammit, someone is always shooting at you."

Abdul laughed. "That is the price you pay for playing with terrorists and other unsavory characters. You won't find us running from a garden party filled with elderly citizens, like those spies in the movies. Those guys are a bunch of wimps. They would not know what to do with a bad guy if he bit them in the arse."

Tillie rolled her eyes. She had met one of the actors who

starred as a secret agent once. He was a nice guy, just not particularly bright. Sophisticated and debonair, but definitely the kind of man who would need rescuing.

She turned to Lady Annabelle, who was huddled in her seat. Her eyes were as big as saucers.

"Can I help you with anything, Lady Annabelle?"

The women's eyes focused on Tillie, but she said nothing.

Tillie tried not to stare. The woman's face was almost grotesque. It was difficult to tell what was temporary and what was permanent. Tillie tried again. "Is there anything I can do to make you more comfortable?"

Anger entered Lady Annabelle's eyes. She glared at Tillie, then sat up stiffly. "I shall need something to cover my head when we land. We have to keep the royal monster out of the public eye, you know. I am sure Aunt Lilabet would be horrified if the tabloids caught wind of this." Her hand swept over her face and body. "It would not be wise to expose my face to the world." Her words were tinged with bitterness.

Tillie studied Lady Annabelle's face. Her words were somewhat distorted, but not difficult to understand. "Actually, some of your *enhancements* appear to be temporary."

"What do you mean?"

Tillie pointed to Lady Annabelle's hair. "May I?"

Lady Annabelle blinked. Finally, she nodded.

Tillie reached for the dirty braid that was wound around Lady Annabelle's head. She felt around for clips or pins. When she found them, she pulled them from the braid and allowed it to fall free. The faux cow ears—attached to the braid—fell with it. Patiently, Tillie removed the ears and placed them in the evidence bag that held the hooves and glove, then finger-combed through the plaited hair, releasing Lady Annabelle's fine blond hair. "A little wash and your hair will be back to normal."

Lady Annabelle shook her hair out. "I was worried they

were going to shave my head and attach a wig. Once they put those gloves on my hands, I could no longer feel what was real and what was not. What about my ears?" She tugged at one. "They seem to be missing—"

Tillie pushed some of the hair away from the area where an ear should have been. The lobe had been trimmed around the canal. The rest of her ear was pinned to the skull and somehow flattened. She withheld a gasp. Obviously, some sort of plastic surgery would be required to rebuild and re-shape her ears. "They appear to have been somewhat surgically altered. Nothing that cannot be corrected, though. How is your hearing?"

Lady Annabelle shuddered. "Just fine. I heard everything those bastards said. About what they were going to do to me, what they wanted to do with me, and how they intended to do it. I learned to shut it out. For a while, I was medicated, but then someone said it would affect my milk production, so they stopped. Then they kept me in line with fear. One of those men fancied himself a whip master." She shuddered, then closed her eyes and appeared to be drifting off to sleep.

Quickly, Tillie spoke. "I *am* sorry for what you were subjected to, ma'am. It must have been horrible." Tillie patted her hand. "But I do have one more question. Who are *they*? Who did this to you? Who kept you prisoner?"

Lady Annabelle's eyes flew open. Then they closed. Finally, she muttered, "I have no earthly idea . . ."

"Ma'am?"

Lady Anabelle yawned. "I am so sleepy. So sleepy. I need to rest." She slumped in her seat and whimpered, apparently feigning sleep.

Tillie gazed at Abdul, her eyebrows raised. She mouthed *What the fuck?*

Abdul shrugged and mouthed *Later.*

The helicopter was still over the Irish Sea when another

copter appeared behind them.

Harvey grunted. "It appears we have visitors."

Tillie turned and tried to get a glimpse of the passengers. "Maybe it's a royal escort." She stared at the aircraft. "Can you see the markings?"

Harvey pulled their copter to the right. "Not unless the Queen's service wears frog suits and carries guns. Dammit. You people attract villains like flies."

Sparks of fire shot out of the guns aimed at them. "Duck!" Abdul gestured with his hands. "They are shooting at us. Evade and scoot."

Tillie groaned. While evasive tactics were required, being tossed about midair always left her stomach in a jumble. More than once, the result had been unpleasant. That was why she had enlisted in the Royal Navy, not the Air Force. She wasn't a horrible flyer, but she was not cut out for the duck and fly maneuvers called for in war.

Harvey dropped the copter several hundred feet and slowed his speed. The other aircraft flew over him, rocking the air. "We need to find a place to set down—and fast. Meanwhile, I want everyone in chutes. You may need to jump." A shot was fired overhead but went wide. Harvey jerked the aircraft right then left, then right again, attempting to avoid the bullets. He again slowed the copter's speed and turned away from the other aircraft. More shots rang out, but nothing hit them. Harvey barked into his radio, "Command? We're taking fire. I *repeat*, we are taking fire. We are under attack. I'm going to try to land, but we need ground assistance, *stat*."

"ACORN Ten C, the Coastguard is almost directly below you. Land aft, on the deck. They'll be waiting for you."

"Negative, Command. If I head to that ship, our pursuers could blow it up. We have *precious cargo* on board, I repeat, *precious* cargo."

"ACORN Ten C, I suggest you splash and dash, then."

Harvey slammed a hand on his dashboard. "Command? How the hell I am supposed to do that? That's like throwing fish in a kettle. A very *small* kettle. We'll be picked off before we hit the water." He muttered, "Idiots."

"ACORN Ten C, then this idiot suggests you execute a duck and tuck and head for Airstrip Eight Niner Tabasco. The Coastguard is sending backup now."

Moments later, another approaching helicopter could be heard. Tillie attempted to view the ongoing battle, but there were too many blind spots in their aircraft. Shots rang out, then some more.

Harvey turned the copter away from the battle and headed to the British coast. There was a loud explosion and the blast shook the copter, but it remained in the air.

Tillie turned and watched a flame-consumed chunk of metal slowly fall from the sky. "Those coasties have good aim. Splunk and dunk."

Lady Annabelle, now awake, shivered. "Bloody hell, I thought we were going to be the ones spiraling into the sea."

Harvey laughed. "Not happening on my watch. Though if you would like to go for a swim, I am sure that can be arranged."

Tillie grabbed her stomach as it took an enormous flip.

Abdul grinned. Then he handed her a plastic airbag.

CHAPTER NINE: UNCOVERING LADY ANNABELLE

Tillie waited impatiently in the conference center of the private hospital. Hospital staff had brought in a pot of tea, but that had long sat empty.

Now, after two hurried trips to the loo, her stomach had settled, and Tillie was ready for some answers. Lady Annabelle had been taken to a consult room immediately upon their arrival, and they have been shuttled off to the conference center. Almost two hours had passed. "What could be taking so long?"

Abdul shrugged. "I imagine she is getting a thorough examination, and after that, the doctors will have to consult with the Queen. I imagine she must approve the necessary course treatment."

Tillie's eyes narrowed. "I hope they don't move her before we can finish questioning her."

"Tillie, we may not have the opportunity to question her. She owes us nothing. The Queen owes us nothing. Technically, our mission is done. We rescued Lady Annabelle. Now, all we can do is wait and hope she wishes to speak with us."

Tillie frowned. "I just want to know how she wound up at the Hucow auction in the first place. We still don't know if she went willingly or was forced. Did she have the ability to walk away or not? We don't even know if what occurred was without her consent. Unless I know how she got there, I can't close this investigation."

Abdul's phone rang. He pulled it out of his pocket, gazed at the screen, swiped at it, and brought the phone to his ear. "How may I assist you, sir?" Abdul straightened up in his chair. "Yes, Doctor. Right away." He disconnected and placed it back in his pocket. "They're ready for us now." There was a knock at the door. "Someone will take us to Lady Annabelle." He opened the conference room door, and a young woman dressed in scrubs indicated they should follow. They did.

Tillie came to a halt at the doorway to a room. A woman was lying in a hospital bed. She was freshly showered and smiling. She looked nothing like the Hucow that had been brought to the hospital. The woman smiled at Tillie and beckoned. Tillie stepped into the room, trying not to stare. She failed. The transformation was almost miraculous. Finally, Tillie said, "I don't understand . . ."

Lady Annabelle giggled and gazed up at one of the doctors. "Dr. Hansen managed to reduce my lips and take care of a few other alterations." She adjusted the sling that held her teats. "I will need reduction surgery for these, of course, but we decided to see whether some of the reduction would occur naturally, since I won't be hooked up to a milking machine anymore." Her hand went to her ears. "And my ears will need reconstruction, but I have been assured that is a minor issue. Great advances have been made in prosthetics thanks to new imaging products, like three-dimensional printers. Apparently, the visual effects were much worse than the reality."

Tillie waved a hand over her midsection. "And what about . . ."

Lady Annabelle flushed. "My internal organs are intact, but Aunt Lilabet is assembling reconstruction experts for the rest. Part of the udder was a prosthetic, but other parts had been altered. I want my body back, so some procedures will be required."

Tillie's eyes narrowed. For someone who had survived a rather horrendous experience, Lady Annabelle's mood had changed dramatically. "You seem to be taking all of this rather well."

Lady Annabelle shrugged. "I am just so relieved to have been rescued. It will take a while before I can sleep comfortably, but there is a reason my family is famous for their stiff upper lip. We survive and we move on. Everything those butchers did to me can be corrected, and that is all that matters." The doctor beside her bed patted her arm and she smiled up at him.

Abdul cleared his throat. "Well, then, may we ask a few questions so that we can close our investigation?"

Lady Annabelle yawned. "While I would love to have a prolonged chat, my doctors felt it necessary to introduce some sedation, but I imagine I am good for a few questions." She smiled at the attending physician. "Dr. Carver, please allow us some privacy." The doctor nodded and left the room. Lady Annabelle gestured to some chairs by her bedside. "Please. both of you, sit."

Tillie sat in one of those plastic armless chairs that hospitals appeared so fond of.

Abdul settled into a large cushioned armchair.

"Can you tell us what happened?' Tillie asked. "How you got to the farm and were taken captive?"

Lady Annabelle stared at her hands. "It was George's fault, really. I was at one of his famous salons, and he insisted everyone try some new club drug he had picked up from one of his suppliers. He assured us it would take us on a bit of a head trip but was otherwise harmless. So, of course, we all indulged."

Tillie tilted her head and inquired, "George?"

"George Danson, the Duke of Sweenington?"

Tillie's eyes rounded. "The MP?"

"The very same." Lady Annabelle waved her off. "I am counting on your discretion, here. He's a friend. At least, I think he is." Her eyes widened. "One can never tell these days." She gazed at Tillie. "Of course, we all sampled the drug, and the next thing I knew we were all flying. Someone thought it a great idea to go dancing at one of the underground nightclubs, and off we went."

Tillie tried to maintain a calm expression on her face. Lady Annabelle was flippantly dismissing the use of illegal drugs and her irresponsible behavior, as if it was acceptable, rather than illegal. Her nonchalance was disturbing. "Go on."

"We wound up at this new place, oh, what was it called? Bubbles? No, Fizz." She sighed. "I'm afraid I can't remember. It was one of those clubs that offers flights of expensive champagne. I am sure you can figure it out." She yawned again. "Anyway, the combination of the pill and the champagne left us all a bit bladdered. I remember putting my head down on the bar to collect myself. When I woke up, I was in a barn with a few other girls, all of us looking worse for wear." She smirked. "Some of them were snoring like midshipmen No class there. Anyway, I got up and started to wander, trying to figure out where I was. Then I called Goo-Goo . . ."

"Who?"

"Oh, George. That's what we call him."

Tillie nodded. "Please continue."

"Well, he didn't answer, and the next thing I knew, some man dressed as a farmer and smelling like pig shit grabbed my phone out of my hands and smashed it. Then he tied my hands and pulled me into a large shower stall." She made a face to show her disgust. "I think it was a place for washing animals or something. It smelled as bad as the farmer. But the worst part was, he threw me in the shower in my clothes." Lady Annabelle's eyes widened. "In a Versace. Who does that?"

Tillie did not respond. She often found the values of the uber-rich repugnant but knew to keep her thoughts her own. "Did he say anything? Did he explain why he was throwing you in the shower?"

Lady Annabelle yawned dramatically. "He told me my uppity snout was going to get me in trouble and I had better learn to behave. I tried to ask where I was and how I had gotten there. He just laughed." Through another yawn, she said, "Then he threw a bag of clothing at me and told me to get dressed. I asked for some privacy and he laughed again. He called me a demanding slut."

Abdul leaned forward and gazed at her. "Did he explain where you were or why?"

Lady Annabelle shook her head. "Nothing. He told me nothing. The guy just kept looking at me like I was a prize heifer, which, I later discovered, I was. The creep insisted on staying outside the shower stall while I changed. I knew he was watching. He was a real perv."

Tillie sat back in her chair. "And then?"

Lady Annabelle's expression changed. Rage flitted through her eyes. "I don't remember. I woke up back at George's. And he pretended nothing had happened." She pushed her hair over her shoulder. "A few nights later, I met Jay Abernathy at a club. I told him what I thought had happened and he laughed at me. Asked me if I had ever fantasized about being a cow. I was curious, so we chatted some more. He invited me to his farm to observe what he called *pet play*. He was hot, and I was curious, so I flew with him to the states." Lady Annabelle smiled. "It was entertaining, and the women participating seemed to enjoy themselves. So, I . . ." She stopped and flushed. "Well, that's a story for another day."

Lady Annabelle muttered something else, then her body went limp, and she emitted a soft snore.

Abdul stood. "I guess that means we have to come back another day. What do you say we pay a visit to the Duke of Sweenington?"

"Parliament *is* in recess. Do we know where to find him?"

Abdul chuckled. "No one hides from MISix."

Tillie watched the MP carefully.

"She's bonkers. I did no such thing. I do not condone illegal drugs and I most certainly do not distribute them to my friends." George Danson, the Duke of Sweenington, pounded his fist on his desk. The office at his country estate was grand and almost, ostentatious. "I knew that girl was trouble. I don't even know why she was invited. She's just one of those lazy royals always hanging around, up for a party." His eyes filled with fury. "I. Did. Not. Give. Her. Drugs."

Tillie instantly knew the Duke was going to be uncooperative. Time for another tack. "Did she come to your party alone?"

Danson glared at her, then his expression softened. "No, she was with that Winston fellow. They call him Fuzzy."

Tillie's eyebrows shot up. Well, wasn't that interesting? She and Abdul had rescued Fuzzy Winston from a white slave cartel in Morocco. At one time, he had been known as a bit of lightweight, but a good source for club drugs. When he was retrieved from the cartel, where he had been servicing men and women to pay off a debt, he had been heavily addicted to GHB, the drug the cartel used to control their victims. Of all of the people rescued, Fuzzy and an American vice-president's daughter had been the most damaged, and required not only treatment for drug addiction, but an extended stay at a private hospital for psychological problems. Both had been sexually abused and broken. "I thought Fuzzy was off the radar. I understood he had withdrawn from polite society."

The Duke snorted. "Believe me, there has never been anything polite about the Winstons. They are all new money. Not a pedigree among them." He stood and began to pace. "Fuzzy reappeared a few months ago. I had heard he suffered some sort of mental problem and was institutionalized." He shrugged. "I guess he recovered or something."

Tillie nodded. If Fuzzy was dealing drugs again, it was *certainly* something. "But Lady Annabelle was at your gathering?"

"Yes. She was."

"Did you accompany her to the underground club they visited?"

The Duke frowned. "Absolutely not. My constituents would not appreciate a Member of Parliament who parties into the night doing God knows what."

"When was the last time you saw her, then?"

"When she and the others left, headed to a club I had never heard of."

Tillie stood. "Thank you for your time. You have been very helpful."

The Duke cocked an eyebrow. "Of course. Let me show you out." He led them to his foyer. "By the way, why is MISix involved in this? I thought MIFive handled domestic matters."

Abdul smiled. "Things are not always as they seem, are they, Lord Sweenington? Sometimes, domestic problems have international implications."

"Ahhh, there it is then." A butler appeared and opened the front door. The Duke shook their hands and turned away. The butler guided them out of the door.

When they were settled into their car, Abdul chuckled.

Tillie frowned at him. "What's so funny?"

"The bastard was all high and mighty about drugs when his pipe was laying on his desk."

"Maybe he enjoys a toke of tobacco occasionally."

"It wasn't that kind of pipe."

Tillie sniffed. "Impossible. No one dares to leave drug paraphernalia out in the open like that. Not when they knew MISix would be visiting."

Abdul smiled at her. "I know what I saw and I know what I smelled. Lord Sweenington may be an MP, but despite his protests, he does walk on the dark side."

"So, turn him over the MIFive. We have a bigger problem."

"The elusive Fuzzy Winston?"

"Sounds like he's back to his old tricks. Guess his stay in that psychiatric hospital didn't take."

"Are you surprised? That man was farmed out like a stud horse. He was pretty damaged when we found him."

"That doesn't excuse returning to his old ways."

Tillie tried to hide her shock at Fuzzy Winston's appearance. He barely resembled the man she had rescued from the slave cartel. The former Fuzzy was well-kempt and well-dressed. Even his full head of red curly hair had been tamed.

The new Fuzzy had undergone some sort of conversion. He was dressed in holey jeans and a wrinkled tee-shirt, his red hair cut short and tipped with blue. There was a small bolt through his eyebrow and a ring through his lip. He looked more South London than Mayfair. Fuzzy was also chain-smoking.

Obviously nervous, Fuzzy smiled at Tillie. "I certainly never expected to see the two of you again. Thanks, by the way. I was in no condition to express my gratitude the last time we met."

Abdul nodded in acknowledgment. "Just doing our job."

Fuzzy sat up straighter. He peered at Tillie, his twitching green eyes betraying his nervousness. "How can I help you folks?"

"Actually, we're here about Lady Annabelle Trask." Tillie sat on the armchair directly across from Fuzzy.

"Annie? What she's done now?" He stubbed out his cigarette but did not reach for another. "I haven't seen her in months."

Tillie gazed at him. "She was kidnapped. She has just been recovered. It has been suggested you might have some knowledge of the events that transpired."

Fuzzy laughed, then stopped. His eyes darted to Abdul, then Tillie. "Wait a minute, she is saying I kidnapped her? That woman is batshit crazy. Trust me, if she is pointing a finger at me, it's because she got herself in a sticky wicket and was caught. What does she claim? That I arranged for her to be kidnapped?" He shifted in his chair. "When was this supposed to have occurred?"

"May of this year. We don't have an exact date." Abdul nodded at Fuzzy's cell phone. "As I remember, you keep a pretty detailed social calendar on your phone. Can you check that month? See if anything comes to mind."

Fuzzy nodded and grabbed his phone. His finger swept across the screen, then stopped. He stared at his phone and screwed up his face. "Any idea who else was there? I'm drawing a blank. As far as I can tell, we shared no engagements."

Tillie studied him. That made no sense. Lady Annabelle supposedly accompanied him. It wasn't difficult to discern that someone was lying. "The Duke of Sweenington, perhaps?"

Fuzzy's eyes narrowed. "Sweeney? I see him all the time. We belong to the same clubs. Play handball, sometimes."

"Any parties at his home, perhaps a dinner party with Lady Annabelle among the guests?"

Fuzzy's eyes widened. "Oh, yes. The infamous dinner party. The one where she put the moves on Sweeney. Freaked the old guy out. She got really handsy. He was having none of it. The evening ended early."

Abdul smiled. "Where did you head after the party?"

"I don't remember." Fuzzy started to shake his head, then stopped. "Wait a minute, a bunch of us went to a nightclub. I think it was called Bubbles, no, Buleax. Crazy place. Lots of freaks."

Tillie nodded at him. "Go on."

"There were a bunch of Yanks in there that night, cowboys. Annie was really on her game. Drinking and dancing up a storm. Got her clutches into some guy, handsome, but older. I think his first name started with a J. Jim? John? Jason? Something like that. Anyway, I got bored with the scene and left. Last time I saw them, he had her hand up her dress and she was measuring his manly pride."

He sighed. "Look, I like Annie, but she's a tease. Sometimes she gets in over her head. She is also notorious for crashing soirees. We arrived at the same time, so I suppose it may have appeared we came together, but I just assumed she had been invited." He paused and lit another cigarette. "Still, as I recall, Sweeney seemed surprised to see her. Of course, he was too polite to refuse entrance to a royal, even one so far down on the list of succession. What is she, two-hundredth in line to the throne?

"Anyway, she was letting it all hang out, as the Yanks are fond of saying. She's a party girl. Who she dallies with is really none of my business." He shook his head. "I haven't spoken to or seen her since."

Tillie nodded. "If possible, I would like to interview the other people there that night. Do you recall who else was there?"

Fuzzy nodded. "Give me your number. I will check with them first, and if they approve, I will text them to you. I don't want anyone thinking I'm a snitch."

Abdul extended his hand and Fuzzy grasped it. They left

him puffing away on his cigarette, a thoughtful expression on his face.

As they walked to their car, Tillie said, "We rescued him from the depths of hell. You'd think he would be more helpful."

Abdul snickered. "Debts of gratitude are fleeting. However, all indications are that he is back to his old tricks. It would be bad business to reveal the names of his clients. Consider his agreement to check with them before turning their names over to us a victory. Because it is. Besides, we can probably get that information from traffic cameras in the area or security footage at MP Danson's estate, even that club."

Tillie snorted. "If it is still available. It has been months."

"Then let's hope luck is on your side."

CHAPTER TEN: LOOSE THREADS

Tillie rubbed her eyes and groaned.

Abdul smiled. He stepped behind Tillie and rubbed her shoulders. "Sounds like you've hit the wall, my love. It's time for a break. An eight-hour one."

"As if I could sleep. This case has taken quite a turn. It appears that Lady Annabelle is not the innocent she pretends to be. And Jay Abernathy, although an alleged scumbag human trafficker, may not have kidnapped her. Nor did he force her conversion to a Hucow. She went with him willingly. The Queen is calling for his head, but I'm not sure it's justified. I need another interview with Lady Annabelle, but I need an interview with Jay Abernathy more. The fact that he is American is a problem. He has no obligation to speak with us, or anyone else, for that matter."

Abdul gently kissed her neck. "Personally, I think it's time to call on our American friends. A bunch of Brits running around Dallas asking questions is bound to create suspicion, and he might run. We need people who blend in to investigate."

Tillie ran a finger along Abdul's face. His five o'clock shadow made him appear dangerous, yet incredibly sexy. Although she was dead tired, she felt a familiar stirring in her nether regions. "I hate to turn this over to the Yanks, but you are probably right. They have connections we don't. And they have been surveilling Jay, so they have the inside track. I suppose I could chat with Dianna. Ask her to assist. He's already a person of interest there. They are the ones who can get closest to him and get the answers we need."

"And we only have few questions—What was Lady Annabelle's true relationship with Jay Abernathy? Were they lovers who ventured into some sort of pet play, or was she a victim? Was she held against her will, or did she participate willingly? Surely they can get that information easily."

Tillie sighed. "I wish there was a more private way to do this, but Lady Annabelle's doctors will tell us nothing. They can't, really. And I don't want to push her without reason. At the same time, I don't want to waste our time pursuing Abernathy unless there has actually been a crime committed against Lady Annabelle. She has to be the focus, not his other activities, as questionable as they seem."

Abdul took her hand and pulled her from the chair. "It wouldn't be the first time an alleged victim has lied to us to cover her rump. However, Lady Annabelle is safe, so we don't need to settle the matter this evening. Tomorrow is another day. Tonight, all I want to do is lie next to my love and get some much-needed rest,"

Tillie laughed. "As if we will indeed sleep." She nudged him with her elbow. "I have not had a full eight hours sleep since I met you. You are like an octopus who needs to be constantly fed. All hands the minute we lie down."

Abdul chuckled and led her toward their bedroom. "I certainly hope you aren't complaining."

Tillie snickered. "Somehow, I don't think it would matter if I were."

Cate Creighton Hazelton slid onto the barstool and waved the bartender over. "Two fingers of your best whiskey and hold the ice." She sighed deeply and tossed her hair over her shoulder. She gazed at the man seated next to her. "Sorry, bad day. Bad, bad day." She emitted an exaggerated sigh.

Jay Abernathy peered at her, interest lighting up his blue

eyes. He studied her, his eyes boldly sweeping her assets from head to toe.

Cate blushed and fluttered her eyelashes, but said nothing. The bartender handed her the whiskey. She slapped down a black credit card. "Keep 'em coming." She picked up the glass, swirled its contents, then held it up to the light. She brought the glass to her lips and chugged it. Daintily, she set it back onto the bar. The bartender rushed over with a bottle and refilled it.

Jay Abernathy's mouth dropped open. He drawled, "Little lady, are you sure you can handle all that liquor? I'd hate to see you fall off that stool."

Cate gazed at him and smiled. As a member of Anders Mark's team at The Agency, she had learned how to hold her liquor—or pretend she couldn't. She was the Agency honey-pot. She could play men like a fiddle. He had no way of knowing that she was a skilled covert operative who could snuff out his life in seconds. The blonde hair, big blue eyes, red rose-bud lips, and a dress so tight it revealed all of her assets, was part of her cover. It loosened lips and turned men like Aber-nathy into braggarts to gain her attention. She forced a slight drawl into her voice and purred, "I'm sure a big strong man like you is more than capable of catching me." She touched his arm and granted him a slight smile. "You look like the type of man who takes risks, which is a good thing, because I am most definitely the type of woman who enjoys risk."

Abernathy's arm slipped around the back of her stool. "Don't worry, darling. I am more than capable of protecting you."

Cate motioned the bartender over, again. He refilled her glass of whiskey and she again chugged it. There were times she was grateful she had been raised in high society. She had learned the art of drinking at an early age. She giggled. "You be sure and do that now." She touched his thigh. "Because I'm going to totally rely on you." She reached into her designer handbag and flashed a keycard. "I'm planning on drinking until I topple." She giggled again. "Make sure I make it back to my room, okay?"

Abernathy's eyes again swept her body, a leer on his face. "I'm your man, darling. I am most definitely your man." He raised an eyebrow. "You must be new to the area. We don't often get fillies of such high quality in here. You a member?"

Cate turned away from him and peered into the mirrored back bar. She allowed a slow smile to turn up her lips. "My ex-husband was a member, *everywhere*. This is one of the few things I managed to salvage from the divorce." She chuckled. "Now he's got a younger, less natural version of me, but I got everything else."

Jay Abernathy's mouth dropped open. "I can't imagine any man dumb enough to dump you, darlin'. Do I know this fool?"

Cate chuckled. "Would it matter if you did? It's not like we're getting married or something. I'm just looking for a way to pass the time." She pointed at his empty glass. "Now, are you going to make a lady drink alone?"

He lifted his glass and took a final sip. "Now that would just be plain dumb, and one thing I'm not is dumb." He waved the bartender over. "Keep them coming, Joe."

Cate grinned and snuggled up to him. "I knew you were going to be fun. Those big blue eyes are all full of mischief. The kind of mischief I don't wanna miss."

Abernathy placed a hand on her silk-stockinged leg. He nuzzled her neck and whispered, "Oh baby, you don't know what you're in for."

Cate heard her phone ping, a reminder that other members of her team, including her husband, were listening. It wasn't easy embracing Marilyn Monroe when your husband was behaving like the Incredible Hulk, but she was simply flirting, not sowing her wares. She got the job done without delivering on the promises men thought she was making.

Cade slid off of her stool and grabbed Abernathy's hand. "Come on, big boy. I want to dance." She winked. "And feel your heat all over my body." She nodded at her drink and said to the bartender. "You can dump the drink, but please keep my purse behind the bar." The man nodded and Cate turned away.

As she led him to the crowded dance floor, she spied Anders slipping through the door. He walked to the bar and shook the bartender's hand. The bartender made Anders a drink and he slid onto the stool next to Abernathy's. He surreptitiously slid something into the liquid, set the glass down, and gazed at others in the bar. Then he picked up Abernathy's drink and left his own. Cate smiled. Soon Abernathy would be crowing like a rooster.

Abernathy grabbed her around the waist and swung her into a Nightclub Two-Step, then a Boot Scootin' Boogie, and a Texas Waltz. Cate was grateful for all of the formal ballroom dance training she had as a child, because the club kept the music varied and diverse. After a half-hour of dancing non-stop, Cate led Abernathy back to the bar.

Fanning her face, Cate asked for a glass of ice water and sipped slowly.

Abernathy downed the glass remaining on the bar and ordered another. "I worked up quite a thirst." He leaned over and kissed Cate's cheek. "This little lady can dance."

Cate gazed at him over the top of her glass.

The bartender set another drink in front of Abernathy and smiled at Cate. "How about you? You done for the evening?"

Cate laughed. "Not even close. Set me up." She turned to Abernathy and held out her hand. "I'm Cate, by the way. I figure after that dance marathon, we should at least exchange names."

Abernathy smiled and took her hand, kissing each and every knuckle. "Jay Abernathy, at your service."

Cate raised an eyebrow. "No way. Jay Abernathy? Really?" She started to giggle. "You have quite the reputation."

Abernathy flushed. "How so?"

"I understand you're interested in some adventurous, uh . . . things. You have a reputation for being very entertaining." Cate paused, watching Abernathy's face carefully. His eyes took on a slight glaze, which meant the drug was working, so she pushed on. "Lady Annabelle, for one. She said you liked to dress her up and . . ."

Abernathy set his drink down carefully and stared at it. "Dumb bitch almost spoiled everything."

Cate tilted her head and stroked his hand. "How so?"

A look of shame crossed his face. "She wanted to be a movie star, but she had no talent, so she decided to go into porn. I have some money in a little ole studio and she wanted a role. Pestered me like a fly on a cow. She wouldn't go away. Finally, I asked one of my directors to take her on. He specializes in fetish films. She went all in. Hooked herself up to a goat milker, had some surgery to pin back her ears, wore weird makeup, and walked around with a tail up her ass. Said she was going to become the next Hucow queen." He swiped at the sweat that emerged from his brow and took another drink.

Cate frowned. That story was so different from what she had been told. She didn't know what to make of it. He had just downed a truth serum. Surely, it had taken effect. "She told me you and she were . . . I mean had been . . ." She waved her hand between them. "You know, were involved."

Abernathy laughed. "That uppity little royal? Not a chance. Besides, what would I want with a woman who had to carry her breasts in a sling to keep them off the ground? She mutilated herself so she would appear more cow-like. I mean, I teach people how to behave like a cow for roleplaying and such, but the mutilation? That's just sick. She was good for a few rolls in the hay, but there was nothing upstairs." He snorted and took another drink. "Dumb bitch."

Cate fiddled with the coaster under her glass. Now she was really confused. Either Abernathy was telling the truth or he was somehow able to fight off the truth serum. She gazed at him under hooded eyes and said in a sultry voice, "So I suppose the part about being sold at auction for millions of euros was all in her head, too? Darn, that was a great story. I really believed her."

Abernathy's face took on a slight greenish tint. He stood and swayed. "I think I'm going to be sick." Then he vomited on the bar, splashing Cate.

She jumped off of her stool. *That was just gross.*

Two bouncers appeared. "Come on man, let's get you a cab. You've exceeded your limit." They grabbed Abernathy under the arms and half-walked, half-carried him away.

Anders appeared at her side. "Did you get it?"

"Of course I did." Cate pulled a phone from the folds in her dress. "This should be loaded with information. At least for our purposes. Not sure it will help the Brits, though." She handed it to Anders and frowned. "Abernathy was telling a much different story than Lady Annabelle. Are you sure that truth serum works?"

Anders shrugged. "It's supposed to be the latest and the greatest."

"Then we have a problem. Let me rephrase that. Tillie has a big problem. I think Lady Annabelle bit off more than she could chew and got caught in a web of her own making."

"But she was being sold at auction, then on the Dark Web."

Cate dipped a napkin in a glass of cold water and dabbed at the stain from Abernathy's vomit. "Some women get off on being sold in a slave auction, you know. It's a great fundraising technique. Sometimes, it's for a dinner or date, other times it may be for more adventurous activities. Who's to say dressing up like a cow can't be a part of that? Hell, those costume stores make great money all year round, not just at Halloween. There's a reason for that. Maybe that's all this is. Some royal getting her kicks."

Anders raised his eyebrows. "I was there. It wasn't a game. Some of those people were really being auctioned off. Sold to owners."

Cate shrugged. "I'm just saying, bored socialites get into some crazy things It could have been just like those bachelor auctions, where people got a day with a Hucow or Hupig or something. Didn't you tell me the only real auction you saw was for those ten people? Maybe the rest of it was just an illusion? A bunch of two-bit actors making minimum wage? They do say all the world's a stage."

Anders shook his head. "No, there were real people made to look like animals in that barn. A lot of them." He ran a hand through his scruffy brown hair. "And the raid. If everything was on the level, why the raid?"

"More drama?"

"They were taking people away in cuffs."

Cate snorted. "Hey, it takes a lot to entertain the wealthy. Maybe that's what they paid for."

"But Abernathy took off with those ten people. Some of them were found chained to their stalls, and Lady Annabelle was found in a cellar on the Isle of Man."

Cate shrugged. "If she's as crazy as we suspect, she could have set the whole thing up. Maybe hopped into that cellar on her own. People see what they want to see. Maybe what Tillie saw was what she was intended to see."

Anders' eyes narrowed. "So, you're saying all of this has been a sham? Abernathy is guilty of nothing?"

"Training women to be a cow or pig, indulging them in

their fantasies, isn't a crime. There are more sordid and more dangerous fantasies being played out every day. And Hucow porn is big." She shrugged. "The wealthier they are, the sicker the fantasy." Cate smirked. "When my mom was the U.S. Ambassador to the United Nations, she was exposed to all sorts of that shit." Cate giggled. "My God, the stories she would tell."

"But she was sold on the Dark Web to a group of Irish terrorists. Surely that wasn't staged."

Cate threw up her hands and laughed. "Again, how do we know that they were Irish terrorists? Did you meet them? Maybe Lady Annabelle wanted to come home, but after mutilating herself, she needed a cover story. So she paid them to play out the fantasy."

Anders stared at Cate. "That's nuts."

Cate grinned. "Not if you *are* nuts."

CHAPTER ELEVEN: THE REPORT

Tillie folded her hands and gazed at the Queen's representative.

"And that is what we have. All of it."

The stern-looking man fiddled with the file folder presented to him and grimaced. "You have failed to state any conclusions. All you have done is offer a variety of statements, but no opinion as to who is telling the truth and who is not. Have you nothing to offer the Queen?"

Tillie gazed at the man and offered a smile. "My assignment was to retrieve Lady Annabelle, not to judge her or her circumstances. I did that. She is safe, back in the Queen's bosom. I have provided the facts as I have learned them. It is not my job to determine who is guilty and who is innocent. My only job was to rescue or retrieve."

The man paled. "You have certainly left me with quite a mess."

Tillie smiled. "I am sure you are quite capable of sorting it out."

The man shook his head. A slight sheen of sweat broke out over his brow. "I was really hoping you would . . ." He withdrew a handkerchief from his pocket and dabbed at his forehead. "I mean . . . how the bloody hell am I supposed to tell Her Majesty that Lady Annabelle is bonkers? Oh, no, no, no. I will *not* be the messenger of such dire news." He gazed at Tillie, his eyes pleading. "Please, at least suggest some conclusions."

Tillie withheld a laugh. She didn't want to tell the Queen

her grandniece might be a pathological liar with an obsessive need for attention. No one wanted to be the bearer of such distasteful news. Still, the Queen had to be told. She folded her hand and studied the representative.

Abdul pushed himself from the wall where he had been observing the discussion with apparent amusement. "Oh, hell, Tillie. I can sense your inner clucking from over here. Stop behaving like such a chicken and throw the man some rope."

"With which he may hang himself, not me." Tillie glared at Abdul. "What do you suggest?"

Abdul sat next to her and began writing on a pad of paper. When he finished, he ripped off the page and handed it to the man.

The man took it and read Abdul's words. "Because the evidence collected is conflicting, and in light of the trauma experienced by Lady Annabelle, we respectfully recommend that she undergo further psychological evaluation to discern the extent of said trauma and the need for further professional consultation."

Tillie could not contain her laughter. "Oh, my God. Who's clucking now?"

Abdul grinned. "At least no one will be moved to call for my beheading." He expelled a sigh. "I shall live for another day."

The representative offered a half-smile. "And so, hopefully, shall I."

Tillie ran a hand down Abdul's sculpted chest, her fingers becoming gloriously entangled in the black curls that covered it. She leaned over and kissed a nipple.

Abdul groaned. "Already? Have you no compassion, woman? After that last round, I am exhausted."

Tillie lay her head on his chest and continued to play with

the black curls that lay there. "Perhaps I need a younger partner. Someone more virile. Better prepared to meet my needs. Someone with more stamina."

Abdul chuckled. He grabbed a lock of her hair and tugged. "Look me in the eye when you cast such damning aspersions, my darling."

Tillie raised her head and gazed at him. "Well, really, our age will eventually become a problem, you know."

"I am only ten years your senior, my dear."

"Yes, but you have already reached your sexual peak and I have not even approached mine. In fact, when I am at my peak, you may be all tapped out. You will be more interested in watching football on the telly than playing in bed."

Abdul grunted. "Well, I could always purchase a cow costume, and you could play Hucow to my farmer."

Tillie grimaced. She plucked at his chest hair "I'm still not convinced that is all fantasy, you know. It appeared to be real."

"Does it really matter? Soon we will have a house full of babies. We will have our hands full and sex will become a distant memory."

"Who said anything about children?"

"You talk about babies in your sleep."

Tillie hit him. "I do not. You are making that up."

Abdul chuckled. "No, I am not. You do talk in your sleep. I can ask you questions and I usually get an answer. Sometimes they don't make any sense, but I can usually figure out what you are saying."

Tillie's mouth fell open. "No way. That goes against my nature. I do not have loose lips."

"Not if you want me to have the information without imparting it directly. I think your subconscious is dying to tell me things you can't." Abdul pulled her closer and began to kiss her breasts. He sucked on both nipples until they throbbed. Tillie moaned. Her body writhed.

Abdul chuckled and moved farther down her body, positioning himself between her legs. "Of course, this always loosens you up as well. A little sweet torture and both sets of your lips become needy. That is when you tell me anything I ask." He leaned forward and lapped at her mons. His fingers slipped inside her and stroked her G spot. Tillie bucked against him. "I'm glad our enemies are unaware of this weakness. It could ruin your career." He pulled on her clit.

Tillie gasped as tiny waves of heat began coursing from her center. This man knew all of her weaknesses, and his crafty tongue was one of them. Abdul could wring every ounce of ecstasy out of her body without breaking a sweat. Normally she couldn't complain about the number of orgasms he wrought, but now he was treading toward dangerous territory. She knew he wanted to marry and start a family. He had made that clear. Unfortunately, Tillie wasn't there yet. She had begun to consider freezing her eggs, so she could put off childbearing and child-rearing for a few more years. At least a decade or so.

Abdul buried his face in her pussy. His tongue licked and sucked, while his fingers continued to probe.

Tillie's brain disconnected from her body. Sensation overwhelmed her. Her body shivered and spasmed as her mind floated off into whiteness.

Abdul moved back up her body and kissed her. Gently, he parted her legs farther and speared her with his cock. He hammered into her, and Tillie rose to meet each thrust. Again and again, he filled her until the white exploded into a myriad of colors. Tillie screamed his name and then she shattered.

Abdul bellowed and filled her. He collapsed on top of her, his cock still inside her, and rolled them both onto their sides. As they settled, he whispered, "Marry me, Tillie. Let's make babies."

You may also enjoy the following from eXtasy Books Inc:

The White House Wedding
Seelie Kay

Excerpt

Sarah snuggled against her fiancé, Sam Charles, and pulled a blanket more tightly around them. She shivered. "Who would have thought the Lincoln Bedroom would be so cold?" she muttered. "That fireplace is too far away from the television set to make a difference."

Sam pulled the blanket more tightly around them. "They probably turned the heat off when they realized we were going to be watching the Packers, not the Redskins." He shifted uncomfortably. "Besides, this settee, as they call it, is hard as a rock. I know it's old, but damn, I didn't think they stuffed furniture with bricks back then."

Sarah giggled. "We'd probably be better off lying on the floor, but then we'd have no way to see the television." She sighed dramatically. "And people think staying at the White House is such a luxury."

"Hey, the food is good. Even some of the beds are comfortable. It's the chairs and sofas and other furniture that are lacking." Sam laughed. "I miss our apartment in Milwaukee.

Everything we have there is comfortable — designed for lazing around in our underwear and watching football. And if I spill my beer or drop some popcorn, no one looks at me like I am defacing a national treasure."

Sarah swatted at him. "These old settees are national treasures, dummy. Some of them date back to George Washington or Dolly Madison. Be happy everything here isn't covered in plastic."

Sam grinned. "No, that would be my grandmother's house."

"Well, after what she told me about your wild childhood, you and those other two hellions you call brothers, she's entitled. I imagine you three left your droppings everywhere."

"Hey! You make us sound like we weren't house-trained."

Sarah rolled her eyes. "I've met your older brother, remember? Every time he visits our apartment, I want to lay down newspaper everywhere. The guy is a slob. No wonder he's not married."

Sam laughed. "Not going there. Be happy I turned out to be marriageable material. Otherwise, you'd be a spinster."

Sarah socked him on the arm. "No, I would have married Mike Carmichael. After all, he proposed first."

Sam snickered. "Third grade doesn't count." A knock sounded at the door to the room. "Come in," Sam bellowed.

Sarah groaned. "Classy, dude."

Sarah's stepmother, Johanna, entered. The tall, lean woman was the picture of elegance. Dressed in a camel designer pantsuit, in appearance she was the antithesis of Sarah and her deceased mother. Where Johanna was dark — with short black hair, flashing brown eyes, and sharp, angular features — Sarah was light. Her blue eyes, long, wavy blonde hair, and soft, round features, made it apparent that she and Johanna were not related by blood. While she had her father's height, Sarah's body had assumed more womanly curves. Emotionally, physically, and intellectually, the two women had nothing in common.

Sarah had tried to find common ground, but her attempts to befriend Johanna had failed. It quickly became clear that Johanna saw Sarah as a threat to her own daughter, Melissa. They now kept one another at a discreet, but polite distance.

Johanna smiled at them uncertainly. "I'm sorry to interrupt, but I wondered if we could have a quick chat?"

Sarah nodded. "Sure, come in. We're just waiting for the Packers game to start."

Johanna sat on a chair next to the settee and carefully smoothed nonexistent wrinkles on her slacks. She gazed intently at them, her mouth set in a firm line. "I know you already refused this request, but I wanted to revisit the matter of the wedding. I don't think you realize how important a White House wedding could be to your father's future. It would be a historic event. Not many presidential daughters have married in the White House. Less than ten, actually. Your wedding would be in the history books. Your children will read about it in school. Please reconsider."

Sam ran a hand through his thick brown hair, his dark green eyes betraying his annoyance. He took Sarah's hand. "We've discussed it. It's just not us. We want a wedding attended by people we love and who love us. We want simple and elegant, and that's it. We don't need anything more. Besides, if I had my way, we'd simply elope."

Johanna blanched. "Oh, please don't do that." Her voice was strained. "Giving Sarah away at her wedding is Jamie's dream. You can't take that away from him." She paused and studied them. "And I don't think you want to deny him his second term as president, either."

Sarah snorted. "Please. It's just a wedding. It should have no impact on my father's presidency or his re-election."

Johanna plucked at unseen lint on her jacket. She sighed. "In politics, everything matters. You don't ignore opportunities. You capitalize on them. A White House wedding would focus attention, positive attention, on your father and his presidency. You can't discount that." Her fierce gaze zeroed in on Sarah. "The publicity alone could push him into the next term. That's publicity we can't buy.

"As much as Americans decry the monarchy in Britain, millions of them get up at ungodly hours in the morning to watch each royal wedding. There is no question that a White House wedding would have the same impact. As a loving and new daughter, I beg you to reconsider. Jamie won't ask you to do it, but it would mean more than you know. Please, do this one thing for him." Her expression was pleading. "I promise that you will have access to the best wedding planners in this country, as well as the White House staff. All you have to do is ask and you will receive. It will require little effort on your part. You two just have to show up.

"Do you really want to see your father lose the next election, knowing you could have done something to change the outcome?"

Sam gazed at Sarah. He placed his arm around her shoulders and began to play with her hair. Finally, he said, "Look, I want what Sarah wants. The bottom line is, if it doesn't make her happy, I won't be happy. We'll discuss it, again, but we aren't making any promises. We have tried to stay out of the political fray for a reason. Our privacy is important to us. Unlike the royal family, we have no paid public role, and we would like to keep it that way. Accepting Secret Service protection was hard enough. You just may be asking too much."

Sarah nodded. "I want to please my father, but we have tried not to let the fact that he is president control our lives for a reason. We don't need or want the attention." She shuddered. "The paparazzi have finally lost interest in us. I don't want to encourage them to further disrupt our lives."

Johanna stood. "All I can ask is that you consider the dramatic impact it could have on your father's re-election." She paused. "And on your career. I imagine a White House wedding would provide quite a boost to both of your legal careers and your law firm's bottom line. And law firm partnerships are offered based on earnings, are they not?"

Sarah and Sam practiced law at the Milwaukee firm of Winters & Simon, S.C., but they had intentionally down-played their White House connection. Both were determined to establish careers that highlighted their skills and not their familial connections. A White House wedding could bring an influx of clients seeking to take advantage of their ties to Washington, rather than their training and experience. That was a big negative.

Still, Sarah nodded, her expression pleasant. Johanna was unlikely to understand their reluctance to highlight that connection. "We will consider it. I promise we will."

Johanna smiled politely and left the room.

ABOUT THE AUTHOR

Award-winning author Seelie Kay writes about lawyers in love, sometimes with a dash of kink.

Writing under a nom de plume, the former lawyer and journalist draws her stories from more than 30 years in the legal world. Seelie's wicked pen has resulted in nineteen works of fiction, including the new paranormal romance series *Donovan Trait,* as well the erotic romance *Kinky Briefs* series and *The Feisty Lawyers* romantic suspense series. She also authored *The Last Christmas, The Garage Dweller, A Touchdown to Remember, The President's Wife, The President's Daughter, Seizing Hope, The White House Wedding,* and participated in the romance anthology *Pieces of Us.*

When not spinning romantic tales, Seelie ghostwrites nonfiction for lawyers and other professionals. Currently, she resides in a bucolic exurb outside Milwaukee, WI, where she enjoys opera, the Green Bay Packers, gourmet cooking, organic gardening, and an occasional bottle of red wine.

Seelie is an MS warrior and ruthlessly battles the disease on a daily basis. Her message to those diagnosed with MS: Never give up. You define MS, it does not define you!

Seelie can be reached at www.seeliekay.com, www.seeliekay.blogspot.com, or on Twitter or Facebook.

www.ingramcontent.com/pod-product-compliance
Lightning Source LLC
Chambersburg PA
CBHW060632130626
46555CB00002B/773